BARABBAS

FELON/FRIEND

BARABBAS

FELON/FRIEND

Marvin Harris

WINEPRESS WP PUBLISHING

ISBN 1-57921-191-7
Library of Congress Catalog Card Number: 99-63452

This book is dedicated to the memory of

Dr. Ella J. Pierce, Ph.D.
Professor English
Mars Hill College
Mars Hill, NC

She told me I could do it. I'm sorry it took so long.

ACKNOWLEDGMENTS

So many people have contributed so much.

Jere and Janie Judd: I was in the mountains most of one summer, writing the story on legal pads. I would send the completed pad to Janie, she would put it on my computer which Jere set up in their house. My mind would race faster than I could write and I left out words. Janie had to figure that out—work far beyond the call of duty.

Peg Cullinane, a neighbor in the mountains and my editor-in-chief. I sent her, in Florida for the winter, the completed manuscript. She sent it back, covered with red ink, with page numbers and corrections spelled out. Such a wonderful lady.

Emma Lineberger, another neighbor in the mountains. She painted a scene for me to place in the book. People have tried to buy the original, but it's not for sale.

Acknowledgments

There are others, in the mountains and in Durham: Virginia Campbell, Betty Youngs, Winnie Wilson, Augusta Hockaday, Mollie Keel, Jerry Williams, Joyce Mitchell, and all those who have asked, "When will the book be ready?"

My wife, who has spent hours alone while I obsessed with writing. Her name is Ruby, and she's a GEM!

And my daughter, Patsy, a silent cheering section, who blesses and inspires me daily. At the last moment she has produced superb drawings of the two main characters, Jesus and Barabbas. A true believer in Him and in me, and who, I am glad to say, takes after her Mother.

And too, the people at WinePress Publishing. My contacts so far have been minimal but most gratifying.

INTRODUCTION

T here is a great advantage in writing the biography of a man no one knows anything about. All it takes is a fertile imagination, plus a lot of time, paper, blood, sweat, and tears.

I told a friend the premise of my story, and she said, "But he was such an evil man!"

We don't know that.

Matthew 27:16 reads: "At that time they had a notorious prisoner, called Barabbas."

Mark 15:7 says: "A man called Barabbas was in prison with the insurrectionists who had committed murder in the uprising." There is no comma after the word *insurrectionists*. Read it again. Who committed the murder?

Luke 23:19 states: "(Now Barabbas had been thrown into prison for an insurrection in the city, and for murder.)" A good defense lawyer would say Luke had misread Mark's account.

John 18:40 simply says: "They shouted back, 'No, not him! Give us Barabbas!' Now Barabbas had taken part in a rebellion."

George Washington, Ben Franklin, Patrick Henry, Robert E. Lee, and Stonewall Jackson took part in rebellions. Were they evil men?

I read, years ago, what I now recall as a filler in *Readers' Digest*. It seems that a tourist was driving through Kentucky, exploring Lincoln country. He passed a fairly long section of old weather-beaten, split-rail fencing. He thought he had seen a sign attached thereto. He stopped, backed up, and sure enough, there was a sign. It stated: "There is no positive proof that Abraham Lincoln did not split these rails."

I lay no claim to being an unerring Bible scholar, but I do believe that, in the Bible, there is no positive proof that the events recorded in this biography of Barabbas did not happen. However, please remember, this is a work of fiction.

Read, enjoy, and perhaps discover—if you haven't already—what role God would have you play.

CHAPTER ONE

Barabbas wasn't exactly jealous but what he was feeling was a bit more than idle curiosity. He kept staring at the man. He didn't know him, and that meant he was a stranger in Nazareth. Barabbas had lived in Nazareth all his life—twenty years—and he and Mary had been herding sheep together since he was thirteen and she was ten.

He had thought that they would someday marry, but then Joseph, a carpenter in the village and thirteen years older than Mary, had bestirred himself. With a whirlwind courtship he had won her love, heart, and hand, and the parents of the couple had recently announced their engagement.

Mary's sheep had finished watering and were moving slowly toward the grazing lands when the stranger, a huge stalwart man, stepped close, put his hands on her shoulders, and was speaking softly but earnestly. Barabbas, unable to constrain himself any longer, signaled to his dog to stay with the sheep and, balancing his staff lightly in his hand, started quickly toward them. Mary, with her head bowed but eyes open, saw the movement and with a slight wave of her hand brought him to a standstill. A moment later the stranger stepped away from her, bowed his head courteously, and strode away toward Japha. Mary stood in apparent bewilderment for several moments, then noticeably shook herself back to her present surroundings and moved slowly off after her sheep. They were quite some distance away and becoming somewhat scattered in their search for grass.

As Barabbas began to draw water for his flock, the dog moved out from his guard stance and the sheep quickly surrounded the watering troughs. Drawing and pouring automatically, he thought of how the events of the past several months had changed his life.

The parents of Barabbas and Mary were distantly related, neighbors, and very close friends. Mary was an only child, and Barabbas was an only son with three older and two younger sisters.

When Mary's parents began to acquire a few sheep, some by purchase, some by gift, and some by natural increase, it was only logical that their sheep should mingle by day with those of their friends and that Mary should be out with Barabbas to help tend them.

Another outgrowth of this situation was that Mary had thought of Barabbas as the brother she had always wanted but never had. Barabbas, on the other hand, had begun to foster a different concept.

As his sisters grew older, there was much visiting back and forth between his parents and the parents of an older boy he knew. Then this boy began to show up at intervals, sometimes for a meal, at other times to just sit and talk. Eventually the two sets of parents announced an engagement. The sister married, left home, and that was that. When this happened three times, Barabbas found himself the oldest child left at home.

Some of his male cronies, having gone through the same process, were either engaged or married and out of circulation. As a result of all this, Barabbas had begun to reassess his own position.

As his sisters married and left home and his male friends were going the same way, Barabbas, without any thought of love, romance, or other emotional feelings, assumed his and Mary's parents would meet, have some conversation, then he and Mary would go from engagement to marriage. Indeed, by virtue of their having tended sheep together for so long, the townspeople made the same assumption.

That was not to be. The unforeseen Joseph had squelched that proposition. To say that Barabbas was disappointed would be a mistake. In fact, he was somewhat relieved. Not that being married to Mary would be undesirable.

But he had seen his buddies and his sister's husbands taking on the responsibility of a wife, home, and children, and he was not quite ready for that. Then, too, there were other complications.

When his friend Benjamin had approached him about joining the brigands, he had jumped at the chance. Barabbas thought in simple terms. His people were ruled by Herod. Herod was ruled by Caesar. Kill and maim enough Roman soldiers and Herod would fall. With Herod gone his people would again be ruled by prophets, judges, or maybe even a king, as in the old days.

To Barabbas and the eight or ten others of the group, it was a simple solution to a simple problem. So far he had neither killed nor maimed any Roman soldiers, but by leading some into traps and ambushes he had enabled others to do so. Moreover, he had waylaid and robbed several unwary and vulnerable travelers of other regions and nationalities, and that was enriching the brigands' coffers, giving them the means to buy more supplies and arms and to range farther and wider into other regions.

But Barabbas knew the unlawful and dangerous activity had cost him. When Joseph began his ardent courtship of Mary, Barabbas realized marriage to her was out of the question. He could not subject her to the uncertain future that he faced. He knew too that his work with the brigands was going to take him away from Nazareth and into the more densely populated areas. He was aware that his parents suspected the truth about his activities, and if they did, others did also. For their sakes alone he should leave Nazareth.

Barabbas saw that he was drawing water and no sheep were drinking. Like Mary's, they were moving off to the pastures, the dog herding them along without being directed.

Barabbas hurried to catch up, impatient to get the flock settled in their routine so he could talk to Mary. They had the visit of the stranger to discuss.

The sheep soon mingled together in their constant search for the sparse grass, and Barabbas made his way through and around them toward Mary, who was on the crest of a small rise, shading her eyes from the glare of the early morning sun as she watched his approach. The sheep paid no attention to his passing. Both flocks were intermingled while grazing and were equally familiar with both shepherds. However, they knew to whom they belonged. While being moved to and from the grazing lands, they looked to their own shepherd for guidance.

As Barabbas strode up the rise toward her, Mary rushed down the hill, her eyes and voice showing excitement, wonder, doubt, and bewilderment.

"Barabbas!" she exclaimed, grabbing his arm and turning to walk with him back up the hill.

"You'll never guess in a thousand years what that man told me."

"Who was that?"

"Barabbas, I can't believe it. He said he was the angel Gabriel, sent by God to deliver a message to me—a seventeen-year-old sheepherder."

"Yeah. If you believe that, then you can believe I'm Joshua and I'm going to make the sun stand still. I knew I should have laid his head open with my staff!"

"But Barabbas, I can't believe it—yet he spoke with authority. And something, somehow, in spite of my unbelief, made me believe. Even when I couldn't believe, it was the strangest feeling. Doubt, fear, unbelief—all mingled and mixed up with the feeling that he knew me, that he was truly sent by God, that I was known to him. Barabbas, what am I to do? Poor Joseph!"

"Of all the stupid sheep crap I've ever heard this is the— 'Poor Joseph'? What do you mean, 'Poor Joseph'? What's he got to do with this?"

"The message, Barabbas, the message!"

Barabbas wanted to shake her until her teeth rattled.

"What message, woman? I don't know anything about a message."

"Remember in the scroll of the prophet Isaiah, it says a virgin shall give birth to a child and he shall be called Immanuel—and the government will be on his shoulders? And he will reign on David's throne? Barabbas, it's what we have been waiting for. That's the message. That's what Gabriel said. I'm to be the mother of the Son of God—conceived by the Holy Spirit. Every Jewish mother who ever had a girl wonders if—"

"But you said you didn't believe it!"

"I didn't say I didn't believe it. I said I couldn't believe it. While he was talking I couldn't believe it in my mind. It's too astounding, too impossible, too—too something. I can't explain it, but in my heart I believed him. My heart was racing and frantic, like a lost sheep among wolves. And I asked him, 'How can these things be?'

"His answer was, 'With God all things are possible.' Then he put his hands on my shoulders, and I had the strangest feeling—a sensation I've never had before. And, Barabbas, then I knew. I knew it was so. It would be as he said."

"What did you tell him?"

Mary replied, "I told him I was the Lord's servant and it would be to me as he had said. Poor Joseph."

"Joseph won't believe this any more than I do," replied Barabbas.

"Barabbas, I'm engaged to Joseph, but . . . do you love me?"

"Of course I love you. I know that, you know that, even Joseph knows that. I expect by now, half the people in Nazareth know it. Mary, you mean more to me than my sisters do."

Mary took Barabbas by the hand, led him to a big boulder half buried in the hillside, climbed up on it so she was face to face, eye to eye, and putting her hands on his shoulders, she asked softly, "And if I'm going to have a baby?"

Barabbas's mind had been in turmoil, racing off in all directions at once, worried about Mary's state of mind, her gullibility. But her question, audible, and her eyes so close to his, brought him up short. He knew this girl couldn't and wouldn't lie. She had to be telling the truth. The only out he had was to go with what he knew: She couldn't be pregnant. So he gave her the only answer she would accept: "Then I would have to believe."

The relief Mary felt showed in her eyes and the tension left her body as she answered, "Thank you, my old friend. Now we had better start tending sheep."

CHAPTER TWO

The next few weeks were more or less routine for Barabbas, watering and herding sheep by day, working with the brigands by night. He and Mary talked little about the visit of the man called Gabriel. She did mention one day that she had told Joseph of Gabriel's visit, the message he had brought, and of her subsequent condition.

"And?" Barabbas asked.

"He seemed calm enough, but I can tell he's having a problem. I'm not too worried though. God wouldn't put me in this predicament and leave me no out. I'm trusting in Joseph; he'll have to trust me. You did."

Barabbas felt a twinge of guilt at the reminder of his declaration, which came from a denial of belief rather than an affirmation of faith.

He was having a problem too. He had seen enough of his mother and of his older married sisters to perceive the change taking place with Mary. She had accepted her pregnancy as an act of God and was serene. Barabbas had not yet reached that point and was definitely not serene.

After a few days of considering a course of action, or no action, Barabbas stopped by the carpenter shop late one afternoon. Joseph had just finished a brace of oxen yokes, swept the floor, and put away his tools.

"Hey, Joseph," he said. "Had a busy day?"

"Yes, and another one for tomorrow," he answered. "Reuben wants a wagon bed built."

"He told me he was going on a trip. I may go with him. But," he continued, "I wanted to talk to you about Mary. She said she told you of the visit of the man who claimed to be the angel Gabriel." Barabbas's voice contained a hint of derision. "I was there you know, and I thought you might have some questions."

"Strange that you should happen by today. I had some questions—some problems. Lost some sleep and messed up some carpenter work due to inattention. I was concerned and embarrassed for Mary in her condition and worried about what the townspeople would think and say. I had thought I could quietly divorce her and send her away secretly until the birth of the baby. But last night it was all settled—no problems, no worries. This has been one of the greatest days of my life. I can sleep tonight!"

"What happened?"

"First, tell me; what did Gabriel look like?"

Barabbas thought for a moment. "Big fellow—big for a Hebrew. A lot of black hair, clean shaven, rough clothes, but clean. A short but heavy staff, and he looked like he knew how to use it. I wasn't close enough to see his facial features or his eyes, but in spite of his huge size and rough appearance he seemed kind, gentle, courteous."

Joseph smiled. "That's the one! He came to me last night—I don't know if for real or in a dream. I told you I had been losing sleep. I had tossed and turned all night, and just before dawn there he was. He called me by name and said to stop my worrying and fretting, to go ahead and bring Mary home as my wife. As he told her, he said the baby was conceived by the Holy Spirit, that it is a boy and is to be named Jesus. Barabbas, you don't know what joy and relief I have felt this day. All this is hard to believe, I don't understand it, but I know it's right, it's true, and I'll be a good father. Maybe I can make a carpenter out of him."

Barabbas had to laugh: first, at the sight and sound of a proud father-to-be with obvious plans and dreams of the future; second, because his relief at Joseph's acceptance of Gabriel's story knew no bounds. Barabbas still did not fully believe. He understood even less than Joseph did. He knew without a doubt Mary was a virgin; she had said so. He knew she was pregnant; he could see. The two facts did not fit any circumstance Barabbas could envision.

His ruminations were interrupted by Joseph's question: "By the way, has Mary told you she is going to see her Aunt Elizabeth?"

"No," he replied, "but she did tell me Gabriel said her aunt is expecting a baby boy. Where does she live?"

"At Ain Karim, just west of Jerusalem. The baby is due in about three months."

"Reuben told me he was going to Jerusalem, and I said I would like to go too. If Mary goes, we had better wait for a caravan. It's about ninety miles and through some rough country. Thieves and robbers all over the place."

"She and I have been concerned how she could make the trip. I'd be glad for you and Reuben to be in the party. Tell me, do you plan to return?"

Barabbas looked keenly at Joseph for a moment and replied, "I don't think so. Why do you ask?"

"I have heard rumors, and Mary says you have been restless, sometimes irritable, and have been taking Gideon out with the sheep."

"I know about the rumors," Barabbas admitted. "I think it's time I moved on. The less you know, or anyone else in Nazareth, the better. I think I have a mission, a purpose—call it what you will—but I don't want to involve my family and friends here at home in some serious trouble. I have heard there is a caravan coming south from Tyre and going to Jerusalem. We had better get ready and go with it. However, don't let it be known I may not return. Better that I should just disappear. Gideon is a good strong lad and can take my place with the farm and the sheep. He will help Mary with the watering and give her whatever assistance she needs when she returns. I'll make it a point to inquire of any southbound caravan about news of Nazareth. If you think there's anything I should know, if you need me in any way, drop a few hints around the campsites. I'll get the message. Use the word *Masada* in some way and mention my name—someone will contact me. Joseph, I love you like a brother, and you know what I feel for Mary. Take care of her, but when we move out with this caravan, let's be casual, like I'll be back in a month or so. No emotion."

In spite of his plea for later casualness at the eventual parting, both were overcome with emotion at that moment. Moving impulsively together, they embraced each other fiercely, each knowing instinctively that since the day Barabbas had witnessed the visitation with Mary of the man called Gabriel, each of the three were bound together in an event that was momentous and unexplainable, beyond understanding.

Mary and Joseph had met and heard the angel Gabriel, albeit a man such as they saw every day, and believed in their hearts that he was who he said he was, and that the words he spoke were from Jehovah God himself. That was the unexplainable-beyond-understanding part.

But how do you explain a burning bush talking to Moses? How did the moving finger write on the wall the message to Belshazzar? How was Elijah taken to heaven in a whirlwind? Jehovah was—Jehovah! He defied explanation. He just *was* and *is*.

Barabbas had had no such meeting with the man called Gabriel. He had affirmed his belief and faith in Mary on that day after her visit from him when she had asked "And if I'm going to have a baby?" But his affirmation was from his head, not his heart. He knew in his heart Mary could not lie to him, nor would Joseph. He had not yet accepted Gabriel as anything but a man like himself. Hence, what he couldn't understand and explain, he couldn't quite believe. He did know, however, that he was a witness to and a part of an event that no one in Nazareth could understand nor would they believe.

Thus, each of the three knew the secret was theirs to keep and that the birth of the baby named Jesus must be a routine, normal happening in the lives of the people of Nazareth. The men released their embrace, each kissed the other on the cheek, and Barabbas turned and left the shop, his vision blurred by tears—some shed for the loss he felt at the distance he must put between himself and his family and friends, and some shed for the quandary in which Mary and Joseph found themselves.

CHAPTER THREE

Before going out to help Mary and Gideon bring in the sheep, Barabbas went by the well where people were wont to gather in the late afternoon, asking if there was any news of the caravan from Tyre. He was pleased to learn that two strangers had stopped by about noon and had said the caravan was only one day behind them.

Next day, there was much excitement in Nazareth. The caravan had arrived, many stalls had been set up, and loud, heated haggling was going on between the people of Nazareth and the merchants and traders of the caravan.

Barabbas made arrangements with the leader, Jacob, for him, Mary, and Reuben to join the group. Jacob was pleased with the additional manpower, for they were going through rough and dangerous country.

Joseph approached Jacob that afternoon, found out what Mary would need in the way of equipment and supplies, and learned that she was assigned to travel with a young couple on their way to Jerusalem. They had two small children and welcomed the presence of additional help with the little ones.

Next day, the trading done, the caravan formed up and moved out, looking cumbersome and awkward to the towns-people but compact and orderly to Jacob and the experienced travelers.

To Mary, it was a fantastic adventure. Having never really been out of sight and sound of the village of Nazareth, she was filled with apprehension at leaving home and loved ones, and also overcome with excitement at the prospect of new friends, new country, and the visit with Aunt Elizabeth. Then, too, she was reassured by the feeling of security she had with the family she was to live with on the trip and pleased with the knowledge that she was contributing to their comfort and convenience. Nor did it hurt to see Barabbas and Reuben cruising up and back along the line of caravanners at intervals all during the day, although she would have been puzzled by the conversation the two men were having late in the afternoon of the first day.

"Reuben, you know how I've traveled with several caravans in the past and reported to you and others on the state of preparedness, weak and strong points, location of quick saleable goods and so on?"

"Yeah," Reuben replied. "You've saved us a lot of time and trouble."

"Well, it takes one to know one. We have such a plant on this job, maybe two men. Have you noticed the two Persians about midway in the caravan, where the goodies are?

One with the loaded camel and the other with the big load on the donkey?"

"Yeah. I talked with the camel driver this morning."

"I saw you," Barabbas replied. "When he made the water stop about midday I had a chance to check the donkey's load. It was nothing but straw. I thought he was too nimble to be carrying such an obviously heavy load. I expect the camel load is a fake too. When they strike, they dump the straw, reload with the good stuff and beat it!"

"I see," said Reuben nodding his head. "What do we do?"

"I've seen this dodge before," Barabbas answered. "There's a gang—we don't know how many—trailing alongside of us somewhere. I expect one of these two will report to them tonight, most likely the camel driver. I'll try to follow, see where and how many there are, and maybe tomorrow we can offer a little discouragement. Say nothing to Jacob yet. Tell Mary at supper that I'm helping Jacob with a lame ox and that I'll eat with him. I'll see you before dawn," he continued, "and tell you what I've found out. And, Reuben, if I don't come back, then alert Jacob!"

From his study of the terrain, Barabbas thought it likely a robber band would be traveling parallel with them to the west, which was fairly level. This would enable them to strike quickly, kill or cripple as many caravanners as possible, load their pack animals, and disappear into the hills to the east. It also meant he could seek a high point on the east side, from where he could see anyone joining or leaving the caravan after they had congregated for the night.

Leaving Reuben, Barabbas continued on to the end of the caravan, stopping to speak with various ones along the way but saying nothing of his suspicions or concerns. Rounding the last traveler with a nod and a pleasant greeting, he started forward, not hurrying but moving faster than the caravan. He also ranged out a little farther to the east, putting distance between himself and the caravan.

When he had worked his way out to where he glimpsed the caravan only occasionally between the hills, he was suddenly startled to find the tracks of another foot traveler going in the same direction.

CHAPTER FOUR

Barabbas dropped like a rock. His heart beating like a drum, his shoulders hunched, expecting a blow to his back or head, he did a 360 degree search with minimum movement. Seeing no one, he slowly raised his head and took a more careful look, especially at the high points.

"Old boy, you have about outsmarted yourself. I think instead of the camel driver going out to report, they are sending someone in. I suggest you ease your way back to the caravan and keep an eye on the camel driver—and if you're smart, the donkey driver too."

Barabbas smiled wryly as he realized he was talking to himself as he often did while out with his dog and the sheep in the rolling hills around Nazareth.

Waiting until he was certain the caravan and the unknown foot traveler were well out in front of him, he got to his feet and warily made his way back to the vicinity of the caravan. Knowing the customary place of the camel and donkey drivers, Barabbas found a place of concealment from which he had a clear view of the encampment, still believing the robber band was to the east. Knowing he needed some options, Barabbas had selected a place that would allow him to move in either direction. The clear sky and bright moon were going to help.

Soon the cook fires were lit, the men brought the animals back from the watering hole, and the smell of cooking food began to make Barabbas's mouth water and his stomach to rumble.

Suddenly alert, he saw the camel and donkey being led back to a camping spot a bit farther out than usual, a cook fire already burning. And now, three men present, not two. Hunger forgotten, Barabbas continued to watch as the men ate supper, talking and gesticulating all the while.

Finishing their meal, the three men arose, walked out a short distance, and soon ended their conversation. The camel and donkey drivers went back to the fire and the stranger moved out in Barabbas's direction.

He had made a good choice for his observation post. The prevailing winds had blown the seeds of the thorn bushes down the slope to his right. Some had been covered in the red clay soil, sprouted and had grown enough to provide cover should he have to move in that direction. To his left, a wadi had developed, deep enough to let him move down hill in the other direction.

Approaching the upward slope of the ridge, the stranger hesitated a moment and moved off to his right, not rushing to get somewhere but neither was he dawdling.

Barabbas dropped down into the wadi and made his way down hill as swiftly and silently as a ghost, raising his head at intervals to check on the progress of the stranger. When he was near the point where his quarry should cross, he slipped out of his burnoose and crouched in a shadow of the wadi, his staff in his hand, his knife in his belt.

The stranger appeared at the edge, stooped, and placing his left hand on the ground for balance, put his feet over the rim and dropped the four or five feet to the bottom. When he straightened up, Barabbas exploded from the shadow, startling the man so that he seemed frozen, paralyzed. Thrusting the small end of his staff under the man's chin so that his head was forced back, Barabbas whispered, "Not a sound. Not a move. Don't make me kill you! Hand me your staff— slow . . . careful."

With his neck bent backward to what felt like the breaking point, the man slowly extended his staff. Still keeping pressure under the man's chin, Barabbas took the staff in his left hand and tossed it out of reach.

"Now, with both hands, open your cloak—slow, slow— and let it fall off your shoulders. Good. Now, the knife. Right arm straight out, two fingers of the left hand, pull the knife slowly from the scabbard—slow. Drop it and move four steps to your right."

Keeping the pressure on, Barabbas moved with him, getting well away from the cloak and the knife.

Seeing a rock formation protruding from the bank of the wadi, Barabbas steered the man toward it until his back was tight against the rock.

Putting his left hand on his staff, never relieving pressure for a second, Barabbas drew his own knife with his right.

"I'm going to take the staff from your throat. When I do, turn around, put your hands behind your back, and try to get your body inside that rock!"

Gradually pulling his staff away, Barabbas moved back a step. Freed from the pressure, the man expelled a long breath and placed both hands on the back of his neck. He apparently was trying to massage some feeling back into his strained muscles.

"Turn around! Hands behind you!"

When he had turned, hands in place, Barabbas used his knife to cut the man's belt. Then he used the belt to tie his hands securely.

"Now, my friend," he said in a low voice, "we're going to have some conversation. I know enough about you, your robber band, and the two Persians in the caravan"—he didn't—"and I'll know if you're lying. I'll ask and you answer. But lower your voice. What's your name?"

"Aaron," a bit unsteadily.

"When did your two friends join the caravan?"

"They were stashed on the route, supposedly out of water, the day before we reached Nazareth."

"Where was the band waiting all this time?"

"We had followed them from Arbel, about five, ten miles out to the east."

"Who's your leader?"

"Demetrius."

The questioning went on until Barabbas had pumped him dry.

"I'm sending you back to Demetrius," he said.

"And the two Persians will join you in the morning, without the camel and the donkey. They will have a message from me and the caravan leader, Jacob. Tell Demetrius to heed it well. Don't move yet."

Barabbas moved away, stooped, and picked up Aaron's cloak and staff. Coming back to Aaron he turned his back from the rock he had been leaning against, untied his hands, and draped the cloak over his shoulders, tying it about his waist with the rope.

"All right," Barabbas said. "Can you walk?"

Aaron swayed a bit, took a few tentative steps, and managed to stay erect.

"Need a drink of water?" Barabbas asked.

Aaron nodded weakly.

Barabbas handed Aaron his water skin, and when he gave it back it was empty.

"Walk down the wadi until you find a place shallow enough to climb out," Barabbas said, handing Aaron his staff.

"Your friends will join you in the morning."

Still a little unsteady, Aaron walked slowly down the wadi, and Barabbas, putting on his own cloak, picked up Aaron's knife as well as his own. Scrambling up the bank, he made his way back to the caravan.

CHAPTER FIVE

arabbas found Reuben sitting by a small cook fire, beginning to get worried about his long absence. Relating to him what he had learned from Aaron about the intent and methods of the robbers, Barabbas suggested, "Let's go see Jacob. I have an idea that may get rid of that crowd."

Jacob had just gotten up, lit the breakfast fire, and was gathering up the lead ropes of the animals to take them to water. Upon hearing of the urgency of a potential problem Jacob rousted out his two oldest boys, gave them the watering chores, and the three men moved away out of earshot.

Barabbas filled Jacob in on his suspicion about the two Persians, how he had checked the loads they were carrying, and of his confrontation with Aaron, their fellow conspirator. Jacob was shocked that the caravan was targeted for assault and listened intently as Barabbas outlined his plan for surprising and getting rid of the two Persians. It was quickly agreed upon, and the three hurried off their separate ways to put the plan in motion.

Jacob walked down one side of the caravan, Reuben the other, each stopping to talk to certain ones Barabbas had recommended, while he went to the end of the caravan and worked his way back toward the center, giving hurried instructions to about eight other men.

Little more than half an hour had passed since Jacob, Reuben, and Barabbas had parted when Barabbas appeared to wander aimlessly into the vicinity of the two Persians. Everyone seemed packed and ready to move and had even asked questions about why the apparent delay. Barabbas spoke pleasantly to the caravanners behind and in front of the Persians, then turned his attention to them.

"Good morning, Ahmed, Faisel. You're ready to move?"

The two looked at each other quickly. Barabbas had never spoken to them before. They smiled and courteously returned his greeting.

"Good morning to you. Yes, we're ready to go and wondered about the late start."

"I've been sent to explain that," Barabbas replied. "Come with me just a moment."

Barabbas turned as if to walk away, stopped, looked back, and waited as they reluctantly joined him. He could sense that they were puzzled and quite alert but so far had no real cause for alarm.

Some fifty feet away from the caravan Barabbas stopped and pointed with his chin.

"See those men out there?"

Until now Barabbas had not looked directly at the men Jacob and Reuben had recruited. When he did, he took a step away from the two, drew his knife, and tightened his grip on his staff. He had told Jacob and Reuben to select a rough-looking crew. His thought was that they had done exceedingly well. It was the most menacing looking group he had ever seen—big, ugly, bearded, and bare chested. They were armed to the teeth with staffs, clubs, knives, and two of them had maces hanging from wrist straps. It was a group Barabbas would like to have had in the brigands.

"See the one out front, just left of center? That's Jacob, the caravan leader whom you've met. The one next to him is Reuben, my traveling companion. Jacob gave me a message for me to give to you. He wants you to go to Demetrius—" The donkey driver gave such a start and a yelp that Barabbas himself was startled. The camel driver didn't turn a hair.

Here's a cool one, thought Barabbas, *and dangerous as well.*

He continued, "Wait a minute. Don't panic," he said to the donkey driver. "I haven't given you the message yet. Besides, you have no where to go. Look behind you."

The two looked, and several men Barabbas had recruited were standing behind them, not unlike those out in front.

They turned back toward Barabbas as he stepped out to face them.

"The message for Demetrius is this! We know where he is, since when and how he has been trailing the caravan, how many men he has, how the attack was to be made, and some of the options he's planned. We are ready, willing, and able to repel any kind of attack. Just tell him that. Look around you, tell him what you see and make your own recommendations. You are free to go—the men behind you will let you pass. Give me your knives, leave your staffs where they are, and do not take the camel and the donkey. Some of the women need the straw to replenish their baby cribs and beds."

Barabbas smiled at Ahmed when he gasped again, and held out his hands for their knives. Ahmed removed his from his belt, gave it to Barabbas hilt first, and turned to walk away. Faisel put out his hand to stop him, turned to Barabbas, and asked, "Your name is?"

"Barabbas."

Handing his knife to Barabbas point first, Faisel spoke quietly but with intensity. "Barabbas, I'm going to remember your name. I'm going to remember this day, this spot, and what has happened here. I will never forget your face. Some day, some where, I will make you remember mine!"

Nodding his head slightly as a sort of farewell, he turned, joined Ahmed, and together they passed through the parted line of caravanners, through their overnight campsite, and without so much as a side glance, continued on their way until they disappeared from sight over a hill.

In spite of himself, Barabbas looked down at the hairs on his arms and hands, each standing up as if reaching for something. A sudden chill went down his back. Never had he felt such a threat.

With a slight shudder Barabbas regained his composure, turned toward Jacob and the men with him, and smiled. Only then did he and the others who had gathered in a show of strength seem to exhale slowly and visibly relax. With a minimum of conversation and without any explanation to those who were unaware of what had taken place, Jacob formed up the caravan and led out. He knew the story of the planned attack by the robbers, the countermeasures taken, and the part played by Barabbas would spread the entire length of the caravan before the noon hour.

Meanwhile, Barabbas took the lead ropes of the camel and donkey left by the two Persians, pulled them out of line, and led them to the couple with whom Mary was traveling. When they learned that Jacob had ordered the animals and what few possessions the Persians had left should be given to them, they were overjoyed and couldn't believe their good fortune.

And as Barabbas had told Ahmed and Faisel, the two loads of straw were a welcome addition to the comfort of Mary and the couple's children.

CHAPTER SIX

The rest of the day was uneventful. Barabbas and Reuben ranged up and down both sides of the caravan and guards were posted that night, but nothing was seen or heard of Demetrius and his band. Barabbas, however, had plenty of quiet time to remember Faisel's farewell remarks and the intensity with which they were uttered. He felt in his innermost being that they were destined to meet again.

The fourth day after leaving Nazareth the caravan reached the vicinity of Jerusalem, and after Jacob had finalized plans with those who wished to return north, the caravan dispersed.

Barabbas and Reuben went with Mary the short distance to Ain Karim, and after setting an approximate date for her return to Nazareth, they saw her safely established in the home of Zechariah and Elizabeth. They then went back into Jerusalem and secured temporary lodging for the night.

The next three or four days were spent sightseeing and exploring in that ancient and historical city.

During this time, by certain secret signs, by a discrete word dropped here and there, Barabbas and Reuben were provisionally recognized as brigands. After many seemingly casual and somewhat inane conversations, each one, separate and apart from the other, was asked flat out, "Are you a member?"

Barabbas and Reuben knew the routine; they had put others through it. The correct answer was "Masada."

From that time on, days continued to be spent learning the geography of the city and its immediate surroundings, but most nights were spent in secret meetings and places with teams of brigands, learning how they were recruited, organized, trained, and functioned as separate teams. Also, how they incited riots and civil disobedience. They learned, too, how the teams worked at stealing from businesses and individuals, and even killing prominent Roman citizens and Jewish collaborators who were considered enemies. Barabbas and Reuben were surprised and elated at the number of members in the movement and impressed with the extent of civil disruption they were causing.

On the other hand, the brigand leadership was impressed with the apparent ability, personality, and commanding appearance of Barabbas and Reuben. Several of the locals had heard and reported in their units the story of the aborted attack on the caravan. Reuben and Barabbas were somewhat heroic already. So much so, in fact, that the leader of the group ordered them not to participate in any illegal activity.

The leadership agreed also that it was far too dangerous for brigands to operate in small towns and communities such as Nazareth. Everybody knew everybody; there was no place to hide, to get lost in a crowd. Reuben and Barabbas had sensed this and each knew that if they were to continue their unlawful activities, they were going to have to leave home. To Reuben, this presented no problem, but Barabbas was in an emotional turmoil. He and Mary had been so close. He had watched over her; protected her from animals, storms, and local bullies; and helped her with lost lambs and birthing sheep. Now she was going to have a baby, and Joseph would be hard put to make a living for three. He was going to be busy; who would look after and protect her? Barabbas knew well enough what Mary would say if he voiced these feelings to her.

"God wouldn't put me in this situation and leave me no out!" But Barabbas felt somehow, down deep within, that he was the out. It was late at night. Barabbas was in bed trying to sleep, and all these thoughts were racing through his mind like leaves in a winter wind. He began to mentally list what he knew, didn't know, what he could do.

Mary is going to have a baby.

Mary said that the stranger said he was an angel sent from God, name of Gabriel.

I saw him, and he didn't look like what an angel ought to look like.

How do I know what an angel looks like?

Joseph saw Gabriel in a dream—or for real—and described him as the man I saw talking to Mary.

He told Joseph the same thing he told Mary.

It takes a male and a female—people, sheep, dogs, wolves, whatever—to make a baby.

Mary has not had sexual relations with Joseph or any man.

Can God, by waving a wand, clapping his hands, by some hocus pocus, make a woman pregnant?

Moses told about Abraham and Sarah. They were old, far beyond child-bearing years, and they had Isaac.

God has always performed miracles—does he still?

I don't know what's going on. I'm as lost as a lamb in a den of wolves.

If God has put Mary in this situation and has given her an out, I'm going to give her one too.

As long as Mary is safe and cared for, I'll work with and for the brigands. If Mary and Joseph—and a baby need me, that's where I'll be.

Barabbas fell asleep.

CHAPTER SEVEN

The return trip to Nazareth worked out beautifully. Barabbas had found another caravan going north close to the time Mary wished to return, and he had gone to Ain Karim to give her the departure date. He had been delighted to see her so happy, rosy cheeked, and healthy. Elizabeth had been good for her.

Now he was looking for transportation. Mary had assured him walking would be good for her, but Barabbas was looking for an out. Seeing a donkey tethered near the temple, he suddenly thought of Hiram. Mary had fallen in love with the donkey left by the two Persians. She had babied, fed, and made a pet out of him—said he looked like a Hiram, so Hiram he had become.

Barabbas remembered the couple Mary traveled with had told him they lived in the lower city, near Siloam. So he headed that way hoping he might get lucky. He did. He had walked streets and alleys for about three hours when he was startled by the loud, familiar bray of a donkey. Staring across the street toward a fenced back lot he saw Hiram's head hanging over the fence, ears cocked upright, tail held high and twitching like a Roman flag in a stiff breeze. Throwing his head back he brayed again, loud enough to set off another donkey nearby, plus several dogs, and a few goats and chickens.

The woman from the caravan came out, recognized Barabbas and greeted him warmly. In the ensuing conversation he learned two things: Her husband was outside the gates of the city sowing wheat in a field they owned and was due home soon; and two, Hiram had been very unhappy. In fact, he had become a nuisance. Her husband had tried to work him in the field, but he wouldn't pull a plow. Hitch him to a cart, he laid down and broke the shaft. Get on him to ride to market, he would buck you off. He missed Mary.

When Barabbas explained his purpose in looking for them he said, "I'd like to buy him from you."

She shaded her eyes from the setting sun, looking for her husband's return, and answered, "The frame of mind he's in he'll probably give you a couple of shekels to take him away!"

Her husband came while they were at the back fence, she talking and Barabbas rubbing Hiram's neck and pulling his ears. Hiram's eyes were closed, and he appeared to be asleep on his feet.

Barabbas received another enthusiastic greeting and, since it was late, an invitation for the evening meal and to stay the night.

Next morning, after a hearty breakfast, the husband left for the field, Barabbas left with Hiram on a lead rope, and nothing had changed hands but a bill of sale for one three-year-old donkey sold to Joseph of Nazareth.

One of the brigands, a prosperous and prominent citizen by day and a master at fomenting trouble for Herod by night, let Barabbas keep Hiram in his stables until the caravan was due to depart.

The day they were to leave Barabbas was at Elizabeth's about two hours before sunup. With hugs and kisses and much shedding of tears Mary said her goodbyes to Elizabeth and Zechariah, and they hurried away. When they arrived at the caravan site and Mary saw Hiram she broke into tears again. Ears twitching, tail flapping, and braying raucously, Hiram upset the rest of the caravan so much that the leader, Jonah, was threatening to tie his jaws shut.

Eventually everything and everyone settled down and the caravan moved out, scheduled to arrive in Nazareth late on the fourth day.

Jonah had heard of Barabbas's exploits on the incoming caravan and asked him to take proper security measures as he had done for Jacob. The return trip was uneventful. Mary walked until midafternoon and rode Hiram until the night stop.

On the morning of the day the caravan was to reach Nazareth, Barabbas scouted twice up and down each side of the caravan and found nothing amiss. Returning to where Mary was striding along with Hiram and chatting animatedly with her neighbors fore and aft, they walked together until the noon stop.

"I won't go into Nazareth with you," Barabbas said. "I said my goodbyes to my family and friends when we left to go to Jerusalem and Ain Karim, and they are not expecting me. I told Jonah several days ago I would leave after this morning scout."

"What are you going to do?" she asked.

"I'm going to hustle back to Jerusalem," he replied. "For one thing, I want to see how fast I can make it, traveling alone. I won't have any stops, I can eat on the run, and I can travel through the night. Reuben is expecting me. We are going in the tentmaking business, and prospects for that look pretty good. Levi, the merchant who kept Hiram for us, has a good-sized storage shed on the alley in back of his market and is charging us a low rent—until we can get established.

"I have here his name and address, and you can get in touch with Reuben and me if you need us. I found out on the trip down and back, and also in Jerusalem, there's a lot of traffic between Tyre and Jerusalem, and it'll be easy to get a message to us. So please, if you need us for anything, any time, get in touch. We'll want to know about the baby."

"I will. I will. I'll let you know when he gets here. And, Barabbas, be careful. Joseph and I worry about you."

Barabbas knew Mary had to be referring to his association with the brigands, but he didn't know what she knew or if she was fishing. Like Joseph, he knew she had enough on her mind with the baby; she didn't need to be concerned about his welfare. He chose to misunderstand her concern. "I'll be careful. If there are thieves and robbers on the trails, they won't be interested in a lone man traveling light. And if they're there, I'll see them before they see me. You take care of yourself, and if the grass gets scarce and the sheep need to be moved to greener pastures, let Gideon take them. You don't have to do it. Take a couple of your neighbors' kids with you so if you should fall and get hurt, or get sick, they can run to the village and get your parents or Joseph. Reuben and I worry about you."

Mary was no dummy. On the contrary, she had always been wise beyond her years. She saw the twinkle in his eyes with his last remark, but she knew two things about Barabbas: He was diverting her attention from himself and any possible danger he might be in, and two, he had through the years been concerned about her welfare and had often given her good advice.

"Get along with you," she said with a smile. "I know you better than you know yourself. Hiram's about to leave me. Give me a hug."

Each held the other in a tight embrace for a moment and Barabbas stepped back, placed his hands on her shoulders, and for the first time in his life, leaned over and softly kissed her—on the forehead.

Turning quickly, he picked up his staff and started walking swiftly away down the line of the caravan that had begun to move the last few miles toward Nazareth. His eyes blinded by tears and his mind in turmoil about when or if he would ever see Mary again, Barabbas neither saw nor heard his many caravanners and friends call to him as he strode by. He moved faster and faster, and by the time he passed the last caravanner, he was running all out—long, distance-eating strides that he could sustain for hours.

CHAPTER EIGHT

Barabbas ran all the way back to Jerusalem. He had a small bag of dried figs, dates, and nuts fastened to his belt and a water skin over his shoulder, so he had no lack of food or drink. He stopped only to relieve himself, and with his tunic gathered under his belt around his hips, he settled down into his mile-eating pace until he reached the outskirts of the city, when he slowed to a walk in order to attract less attention. Looking at the position of the sun, he estimated he had covered eighty miles in about twenty-four hours.

It gave Barabbas a feeling of relief to know that should he have to, he could get back to Nazareth in a day and night. Also, as a young man, he was proud of his physical prowess.

I could give some of Caesar's soldiers a run for their money, he thought to himself as he continued on into the city center.

Needless to say, Reuben was delighted to see Barabbas entering the door of the tentmaking shop. Stashing his big needle, he swept the tent cloth off his lap onto the floor and clasped Barabbas in a bear hug.

"What of Nazareth? Did you see my parents? Did Mary make the trip well? How was Joseph? Is Gideon taking good care of the sheep? Did you have any trouble on the way back? What about . . ."

Barabbas laughed at his big friend and put his fingers lightly across his lips.

"I didn't get into Nazareth," he replied. "We were about five miles out, and I told Mary I had said all my farewells and didn't want, and felt no need, to go through that again. And I wanted to get back here to see to our work, tentmaking and otherwise. Yes, Mary handled the trip beautifully. Elizabeth had told her to do a lot of walking, so she walked until the noon stop, sometimes afterward, then rode Hiram the rest of the way. That donkey is worth his weight in gold."

The conversation settled down to questions and answers on the tentmaking business, then more quietly and carefully on the recruiting and other activities of the brigands.

Reuben said, "Levi has recommended us as tentmakers to several people, and we have a number of orders. And we need to get some goods made up and on hand for people who come in and want something yesterday! I've hired two people: an experienced tentmaker and an apprentice who is quite good, eager to learn. You and I are going to have to learn quick. Our lines of work are going to interfere with each other."

"I can see that," said Barabbas. "Where are our employees?"

"They had to go out on a delivery. We need to find Hiram's brother."

"I can see that too. I didn't mean for this tentmaking to keep us from our main purpose, and I don't believe Levi did either. We'll have to talk to him. I'll learn tentmaking—we need the job for a cover. But I want to get on with Levi in the trouble-making business."

Reuben answered, "Levi knows we have a problem. And, Barabbas, I know you're impatient. You want to start making waves. But Levi knows best. He's been here a long time, and we're just country boys. He says we have to have some sort of cover—it's most important. He says there are a lot of toadies here who would like to curry favor with Caesar's legions by betraying a rebel. His first and foremost interest is to protect us. Go on back to our living quarters and get some rest. Seth and Judas will be back soon. We can work with them for a while, and I'll get word to Levi that we need some conversation."

Barabbas went back through the door to the room Levi had partitioned off for them. There was a kitchen with cooking facilities, both inside and outside in the alley, and a sailcloth partition on a wire to close off the sleeping quarters. Barabbas pulled the cloth open just wide enough to step inside, saw a bed, and that was the last thing he remembered for about ten hours.

CHAPTER NINE

Levi proved to be aware and sympathetic about how the tentmaking business was interfering with brigand business. He was also aware that this was much more of a problem for Barabbas than for Reuben.

Reuben took to tentmaking like a duck takes to water. He had a knack of knowing how, where, and when to buy materials with which to work. Hearing what a customer wanted, he quickly sketched it out, showed the good and bad points, made changes, and made a sale. He could estimate costs, add a profit, and quote a sales price while Barabbas watched in slack-jawed wonder.

On the other hand, Barabbas could cut and sew with the best of them, except Reuben. But the confinement drove him crazy. Caesar's soldiers, for the most part, were tolerant, fairly well behaved, and were respectful of Jewish ways and customs. But they were interlopers! They enforced Roman laws. Jews were God's chosen people and were answerable only to Him. He had promised them a king—long overdue. Get rid of Caesar's minions, and the king—wherever and whenever—could move in with his army, so ruminated Barabbas as he plied his needle and fretted.

Levi had worked with business people and brigands alike for a long time. He knew how Barabbas felt and knew he was a square peg forced into a round hole. He set his wheels in motion and wound up with two assets of great value: one, a profitable tentmaking business that was good cover for whitewashing stolen goods and also could provide legitimate funds for recruiting, training, and arming more soldiers for the new king's army. And two, Barabbas was a master at recruiting and training.

When he wanted to be, he was affable, humorous, loquacious, and a good listener. Sitting in a crowd around any gate of the city, he would soon be surrounded by a number of men. After an hour or so of conversation—serious or somewhat ribald—one or another would squint at the sun and begin to take his leave. From listening to conversation and having made judgements and assessments, Barabbas would casually say, "I was about to leave too, and I'm going your way. I'll walk with you." And off the two would go, Barabbas and another possible recruit.

So both businesses, tentmaking and brigands, began to flourish.

Late in the year Barabbas was at the main gate of the city, holding court as usual when four Roman soldiers rode up with a flourish and clatter. Two dismounted and walked toward the gates as the other two blew loud blasts on trumpets. Seeing they had the attention of everyone present, the two mounted soldiers, back to back, facing in and out of the city, shouted: "Hear Ye! Hear Ye! Hear Ye! Notice is hereby given. By decree from Caesar Augustus, a census is to be taken of all the Roman Empire. Take due notice hereof, and act accordingly. Read the proclamation."

The two soldiers on foot swung the city gates away from the walls so they had access to both outer and inner surfaces. Using the hilts of their swords as hammers they nailed copies of the proclamation to each side of each gate, so that when the gates were open or shut, people inside or outside the city would see the decree. Having done this, the two soldiers re-mounted and the four rode away.

Never one to miss a trick, Barabbas strolled toward one of the notices.

"Let's see what Caesar's going to have old Herod do now to make our lives miserable," he said in a loud, derisive tone of voice. "Take a census, huh? Probably thinking of drafting some Hebrews into his army!"

Caesar was prohibited by Roman and Jewish law from putting Jews in his army legions, and Barabbas knew it. He also knew the value of the "big lie" rumor. Before sunset, word would spread over Jerusalem that Caesar, or Herod, was about to force Jews into his armies.

I'll be recruiting some Jews for my army, thought Barabbas. But while that thought went through his mind, another crowded it out.

Mary! Joseph! The baby!

The proclamation stated that the people were to register in "their city." Mary and Joseph, as was Barabbas, were of the line of David. This meant that they would go . . . where? To Bethlehem!

As Barabbas elbowed his way through the crowd with many of them muttering imprecations about Caesar's armies, he came near enough to read the date of the required registration. Muttering curses of his own, Barabbas began to count on his fingers. Mary and Joseph would be lucky to get to Bethlehem before the baby came. And how about his parents? They weren't getting any younger. How could they make the trip?

His mind getting chaotic with ifs, buts, and whens, Barabbas forgot his recruiting possibilities and set off at a trot for the shop and Reuben.

On entering the shop Barabbas saw that Reuben had already heard the news. He was seated at his bench, a piece of cloth in one hand, a threaded needle in the other, staring at both but seeing neither. Greetings from Seth and Judas roused him from his deep study, and he greeted Barabbas with a rueful smile.

"Well, what do we do now?" he asked.

"We can't stop the tentmaking," Barabbas replied. "We'll put the other business on hold. I think I had better go to Nazareth and come down with our parents—and Mary and Joseph. The baby's about due, and she'll have a hard time making the trip."

"Speaking of babies," Barabbas continued, "I heard several weeks ago that Mary's Aunt Elizabeth had her baby."

"Was it a boy?"

"Yeah, and he caused quite a stir. An angel, I don't know if it was Mary and Joseph's angel, had told them it was coming. Zechariah had some doubts and was struck dumb. Couldn't say a word. After the boy was born, the family—aunts, uncles, cousins—were gathered 'round arguing about a name for the kid. Zechariah came out of the temple and announced in a loud voice that 'his name is John!' That shook 'em up," Barabbas finished with a laugh.

"I'll bet it did," chuckled Reuben. "Yes, I think you had better go to Nazareth and come down with the folks. There will be such a crowd, I don't think there will be any danger from robbers. But you'll be a big help with the stock, cook fires, and kids. I've noticed how kids around here take to you. How much time do we have?"

"Not too much," answered Barabbas. "About two weeks. With a group that big and with people joining up along the way, it will move slow. Probably be a five- or six-day trek. I've got some loose ends here to take care of. I'll go see Levi now and let him know what's going on. There was a lot of excitement about as I came through the city."

"I heard a lot of commotion around the temple this afternoon when the soldiers put up the notices over there. I sent Judas over to see what it was all about. He came back and said Caesar was about to draft us into his army."

Barabbas smiled but made no reply.

CHAPTER TEN

L ater in the afternoon Barabbas went to see Levi. He explained he would have to take leave of the brigands in order to help his and Reuben's elderly parents get to Bethlehem, and also Mary and Joseph.

"Oh, yes, I remember her. We kept her donkey in our lot for a day or so—a mighty stubborn jackass as I recall."

"Stubborn is right," Barabbas agreed. "With anyone but her. I think she can make him lie down and roll over."

Barabbas then told Levi how he had started the rumor that morning about Caesar looking for Jews for his army and also what Judas had heard around the temple.

"It may bring us some recruits," said Barabbas, "plus foment trouble for Herod!"

"Trouble for Herod I can appreciate," answered Levi. "The more the better. As for recruits, I'm not so sure."

"What do you mean?" asked Barabbas.

"Well, you know we have a lot of riff-raff hanging around the city, especially around the gates and the temple area. Most people when they stop to think, know that Caesar can't enlist Jewish people. But this riff-raff doesn't stop to think, and if they were members of the brigands, they still wouldn't. Put one of them in prison, tighten the screws a little, and he would spill his guts.

"The council met at noon today and after a lot of discussion, decided we must be a little more selective. Perhaps it's a good thing that you are going to lay low for a while. The centurion got close to us on that killing last week. We've ordered a temporary shut down for a few weeks. Go back to Nazareth and see that your family and friends get safely to Bethlehem. Spread all the anti-Herod rumors you can, but don't bring any suspicious attention to yourself or to the brigands. See me when you get your people registered and back to Nazareth. Then we'll see how the wind blows."

Barabbas could not help but agree with Levi's assessment of the situation and hurried back to the shop to report to Reuben on the conversation. They both agreed that Reuben should stay with the tentmaking and Barabbas should return to Nazareth and see that the Nazareth people made it to Bethlehem safely and on time.

Barabbas spent the next day tying up loose ends of his tentmaking and his cell connections, all of which were numerous. He also went to Ain Karem to get a report on Elizabeth, Zechariah, and baby John. The baby was about six months old, growing and gurgling as did all babies Barabbas knew anything about. While there, he looked at father, mother, and child but could see no resemblance to either parent in the child. This thought made him realize that while sewing canvas for sails and tents or walking the streets of Jerusalem, he had often wondered who the baby Jesus would look like. With a wry smile he thought, *Lord, I hope he looks like his mother!*

Next morning Barabbas ate breakfast with Reuben, waited a little past sun up until Seth and the lad Judas showed up, bade them all goodbye, and made his way through the awakening marketplaces toward the north gate. He had no reason to try to set a speed record on his journey, so when he caught up with a small party going in his direction, he matched his pace with theirs. They traveled together that day and the next.

Barabbas had thought the third day would be at a leisurely pace also, but at about the noon hour he began to realize that if he ran on alone he could reach home by sundown. Spurred on by the idea of seeing his family and friends, he told his newfound companions of his feeling of urgency. He told them good luck and Godspeed, and was soon out of their sight.

There was rejoicing in many of the homes in Nazareth that night. Barabbas had a big family and a lot of friends. Even though his immediate family had sat down to a simple meal, his mother had the waning cook fires stoked up. She set the girls to preparing a feast and sent the younger children off through the village to spread the news of Barabbas's return and to invite relatives and friends to the celebration.

CHAPTER ELEVEN

Barabbas thought he had never had it so good.

His and Reuben's families were particularly glad to hear of the success of the tentmaking business. Each family had heard bits and pieces of the brigand rumors and had spent many uneasy hours worrying about their boys. It was with great relief that they assumed the tentmaking was so successful that it took all their time, energy, and interest. The few brigands who were still in Nazareth were somewhat aware of what was going on and were circumspect enough to avoid raising any semblance of suspicion to themselves, Barabbas, or Reuben.

The celebration and feasting went on into the wee hours of the morning, and Barabbas was keenly aware of the absence of Mary and Joseph. When the last celebrant had said goodnight and gone home for what would be a short nap before rising again, Barabbas asked his mother, "What's going on with Mary and Joseph? Why weren't they here?"

"A baby is what's going on with Mary and Joseph," she answered. "She's big as a cow! That's right. You didn't know that, did you? She was pregnant when you and Reuben left here with her going to Elizabeth's. We didn't know it then. It was a near thing, with her betrothal and all. Some little bit of gossip and speculation but not too serious. She's doing all right I guess. Goes out with Gideon and the sheep most every day. Comes in about noon. The midwife tells her to keep active—walk a lot. Some of us wonder if she'll make it to Bethlehem. . . . And that's another thing: The midwife is not of David's line, and she won't be going to Bethlehem. But is Mary worried? Not her! She's calm, serene, cool as a cucumber. You'd think she was still fifteen and herding sheep. Not a care in the world."

As his mother rattled on, Barabbas realized with a start that only he, Mary, and Joseph knew about the visits of the man who called himself Gabriel. And if there was a bit of speculating and gossip, a near thing with their betrothal, what would have been said if the people of Nazareth were told the story that Mary related to him on the hillside in the outskirts of Nazareth that day long past? The couple, plus their families, would have been laughed out of town. They would have to go to a city like Jerusalem and try to lose themselves there. And even then, a story that wild would no doubt follow them.

"Barabbas, are you listening to me?"

He jumped as his mother's voice brought him back to the present.

"Yeah, yeah, I'm listening."

"So what did I say?"

Caught, Barabbas gave his mother a rueful smile. "I don't know. At the time, I was back in Jerusalem."

"That's what I was talking about," she replied. "I always wanted Mary as a daughter-in-law. I asked you if you and Reuben would have gone to Jerusalem earlier and got into tentmaking, if Mary would have married you instead of Joseph."

"No, Mama," he answered. "I saw that handwriting on the wall a long time ago. Mary's feelings toward me have always been brotherly, not husbandly, if that's a good way to put it. She's always thought of me as a big brother. We've talked a lot. She's been curious, asking a lot of questions. I expect we have had discussions, talked about things she hasn't mentioned to her parents. Things she just wouldn't acknowledge in a conversation with a man she thought she would marry."

"Like what?"

"Well," he said tentatively, "like herding sheep, for instance. She has been out with me and sheep since she was ten years old. She has seen rams and ewes breeding. She has seen ewes getting heavy and slow. She knows them by name, and she asks questions. She has seen lambs being born, and sometimes her father or I have to help them. She has seen sheepdogs breeding and puppies born. She asks more questions. She sees newborn babies—in her family and ours—and she asks more questions. God knows I'm no expert. My knowledge is limited to animals and how that relates to humans. From my answers to her questions, veiled and sprinkled with 'I don't knows' and 'I'm not sures,' I suppose she's able to relate all this to people also.

"Say, have you talked to my sisters about all this stuff?"

"No-o-o. Not really. And my mama didn't talk to me about it either. Nor did I have a big brother friend I could talk to. Maybe I had better send the younger girls out herding sheep!"

"No, don't turn them over to just anybody. You had better go with them and do the explaining yourself."

Barabbas looked at his mother and smiled. He knew he had made her uncomfortable. He had been uncomfortable himself, talking with Mary about such things but had tried not to show it. And now, with the imminent birth of her baby boy, Jesus, he was glad he had given her some inkling of what to expect.

Putting the last of the food and the dishes away, Barabbas gave his mother a hug and a kiss and started to bed.

"Barabbas?"

He stopped, turned and looked at her inquiringly. "Yes?" he asked.

She hesitated.

"About your work in Jerusalem—tentmaking, . . . whatever. Are you likely to get into any serious trouble?"

The one question he had dreaded and had hoped to avoid. He could lie and dissemble, deceive and reassure her. But if he did get in serious trouble, her hurt would be even deeper and more unbearable. He had to face the truth and she did too.

"It's not likely, Mom, but possible. I'm sorry, but it's something I feel I have to do."

She turned her back. Barabbas knew it was to hide her tears. "I understand. I just have to ask of you, please be careful. A mother worries. Now go on to bed."

Barabbas turned and quietly left with the thought, *A son worries too.*

CHAPTER TWELVE

"Hey, Joseph," exclaimed Barabbas as he entered the carpenter shop about midmorning next day.

"Barabbas!" called Joseph as he jumped to his feet, spilling carpenter tools and pieces of wood across the floor. "How's the rich tentmaker this morning?"

Breaking from an embrace they stepped back and looked at each other.

"Stuffed, sleepy, and certainly not rich," answered Barabbas. "How did you come by 'rich'?"

"Half the village has been in here this morning, telling me what a feast we missed at our rich, tentmaking neighbor's house. I took it all with a grain of salt. They think I'm a rich carpenter!" Both men laughed. Barabbas pushed the door shut, and they sat down near the stove for the nights were beginning to get chilly and mornings slow to warm up.

They began to catch up on the past seven or eight months, and then Joseph began to show his friend what he was currently working on: chairs—both high and low—a crib, a bed, toys, and a wagon in which Mary could bed down the baby and pull to market. She could even take it out to the grazing grounds with the sheep. Listening with faint amusement and a tinge of envy at such an overt demonstration of joy and happiness, Barabbas saw a shadow fall across the room. He looked up and saw Mary, both hands on each side of the doorframe, pulling herself up the one step into the shop. He had thought his mother had prepared him, but no, not for this. The young, slim, lithe, Jewish girl, going out with the sheep every day except the Sabbath, drawing gallons of water from a well, moving quickly and surely up, down, and across hill and dale, bringing lost lambs to anxious mothers, helping with birthing ewes, squatting, sitting, kneeling, running. Where was she? Not this girl! Not this—woman: spine arched backward, trying to compensate for the load out front, trim ankles swollen, movements slow and awkward.

As Barabbas stared in open-mouthed disbelief, Mary stopped, put her hands on whatever hips she could find, and said plaintively, "Well, you've got a mother and father, married sisters. You know everybody in the village. Haven't you ever seen a pregnant woman before?"

At the burst of hearty laughter from Joseph, Barabbas snapped shut his hanging jaw and gave a weak grin. When Joseph released his young mother-to-be, Barabbas moved in and gave her a careful gingerly hug.

Putting the palms of her hands against his chest she pushed him slightly away, tilted her head back so she could look into his eyes, and said softly but clearly, "I'm tough. You made me tough. I won't break. Now give me a hug!"

Barabbas gave her another hug, better this time, and from the beating of her heart against his he felt all the love, appreciation, trust, and devotion she had had for him through the years. He knew from the depths of his being that this girl, this woman, would be a very special mother to a very special baby.

Pushing him away again she looked up, saw tears in his eyes, looked at Joseph, and saw him knuckling at his eyes. She moved off through the shop to the back door, saying over her shoulder, "Give me half an hour, and you babies come on to the house for lunch." And when she was through the door, out of sight, she wiped her own eyes on her sleeve.

After lunch the three continued to sit around the table discussing the upcoming trip to Bethlehem. Joseph had made a two-wheeled cart and fashioned a yoke and harness, with the intention of having Hiram pull the rig laden with the household and baby necessities they would need. Trying it out one day, primarily to see if the cart and harness worked together, Hiram had promptly kicked the whole thing to pieces. Joseph immediately began looking through the wreckage for a piece big enough to use as a club and was looking from the club to Hiram and back to the club when he became aware of the laughter. Looking around he saw Mary, bent as double as she could bend at the time, holding her sides, and tears of laughter streaming down her cheeks. Near her were her father and mother, hanging on to each other, and nearby were several other friends and neighbors, all convulsed with laughter.

Realizing what he must have looked like when Hiram destroyed the cart, then his hurried search for a club—picking up and discarding piece after piece until he came upon one that seemed adequate—Joseph dropped his club and hung on to the side of the carpenter shop. He too bent over and laughed uncontrollably. Meanwhile Hiram seemed to be asleep on his feet.

Hearing this story and picturing Hiram and Joseph in his mind, Barabbas had a big laugh along with the other two.

"I built another cart," Joseph said, grinning, "and traded some work for an ox. Tried him out, and he seems pleased to have such a light load."

"He and Hiram get along well too," Mary explained. "They even sleep together."

Getting back to the Bethlehem trip, Barabbas learned that the villagers planned to leave the second day hence. And as far as Mary and Joseph were concerned, all was in readiness.

"What about the baby?" Barabbas asked. "When is he due?"

"Anytime," answered Mary.

"We haven't seen or heard anything else from Gabriel," said Joseph. "Not since he appeared to me. And Mary is not too concerned. In fact, not at all."

"What if he's born on the way?" Barabbas asked.

Joseph spread his arms and the palms of his hands in a gesture of resignation.

Mary replied, "You know how I feel, in my mind I mean: This is God's child," patting her stomach and holding both hands pressed softly against the sometimes gentle, sometimes not-so-gentle movement inside. "He was promised a long time ago. Whenever and wherever it happens, God will see that Jesus is protected, safe, and taken care of. With my mother, Joseph, you, and Him, I don't worry."

"But what about you?" said Joseph and Barabbas in the same breath.

"He took care of Ruth and Naomi. He took care of Esther. Put yourself in His hands, He takes care of you. You may have trials, may suffer. May even die. But He *does* take care of you!"

A *woman's logic*, thought Barabbas. *What can you do?*

CHAPTER
THIRTEEN

T wo mornings later the caravan moved out.
Having heard from Mary the story of how Barabbas
had sniffed out the plan of the two thieves and saved
the earlier caravan from attack, Barabbas had been unani-
mously selected and elected as caravan leader. Although he
had expected to be free of any such responsibility so he could
stay near his parents, Mary, and Joseph, he agreed to accept
the leadership role. Seeing his hesitation and sensing the reason for it, the family first in line suggested they swap places
with Mary, Joseph, and their parents. With that situation
taken care of, the caravan was on its way.

Before leaving Jerusalem for Nazareth and thinking ahead
about the trip to Bethlehem, Barabbas had assumed it would
be a four-day trip—about twenty miles a day. He set a fairly
slow pace in deference to some of the older people on the

trek. Two conditions changed his mind before noon. The first: Barabbas smelled snow in the cold wind that blew down out of the hills to the northeast; and two: He was thinking of Mary's answer of "anytime" to his query as to when would the baby be born. To Barabbas it looked as if "anytime" could be the next hour!

Using a possible snow as an excuse he set a fast pace. With all the hullabaloo of getting the group together, animals and children settled in and excitement eased off, places designated, and a myriad of other details worked out, it was about midmorning when they left Nazareth—two hours late in Barabbas's opinion.

Mary had walked for over an hour, but the fast pace had about done her in. She was now riding Hiram, sitting sidesaddle with an improvised backrest.

By the time he called for the noon rest stop Barabbas had all the excuse for haste he wanted. It had gotten colder, the clouds were lower, and a smattering of snowflakes was falling. Walking down and back up the line of marchers Barabbas sensed a feeling of urgency in everyone. They were hurriedly watering and feeding the animals and children, and were themselves eating at the same time. As Joseph attended to Mary's needs, Barabbas led Hiram off to one side and saw that he was fed and watered.

"Hiram, listen to me," he said quietly as he gently rubbed him down with a piece of canvas. "I hope you know what a precious load you're carrying. Watch your feet; don't you dare stumble."

Working quickly and talking softly all the while, Barabbas rubbed his back, head, ears, sides, legs, and belly. Hiram's skin rippled with pleasure as he did so. Rubbing his head and ears again, Barabbas repeated, "Mind me now; watch your step." Moving back a bit, Barabbas was surprised to see that, while he was usually seemingly asleep on his feet, Hiram was bright-eyed and bushy-tailed, alert and ready to go. Turning to lead him back to the lineup he was somewhat startled to see Mary and Joseph standing there, broad smiles on their faces.

"Who are you talking to?" Joseph asked.

"I've been rubbing down and talking to Hiram," he replied. "And you know, I think the jackass understands me."

A sharp jolt into his back and a loud, raucous bray from Hiram almost knocked Barabbas off his feet.

"What's the matter with that dumb brute?" Barabbas asked wrathfully, having trouble keeping his balance.

"He's not a dumb brute," Mary answered with a laugh. Putting an arm around Hiram's neck and her cheek against his forehead, she continued, "He's a smart brute. And he's telling you he's a donkey, not a jackass."

"Well, let's get you on this smart donkey and get moving," said Barabbas. He and Joseph picked her up, made her as comfortable as possible, and with a loud, "Let's go!" the caravan was on its way again.

Barabbas did not call a halt until it became too dark and too dangerous to safely travel the rough trail.

The snow flurries had been intermittent all afternoon. Joseph and Barabbas quickly set up tents for each of their families and built one cook fire for both. Then Barabbas left to walk the line to see that the animals, and then the people, were properly cared for.

Getting back to the head of the line he saw Joseph feeding and watering the ox. So he walked up to Hiram and, warily giving him a playful slap on the rump, asked, "How's the donkey doing?"

Turning and pushing his head gently into Barabbas's stomach he turned sideways, flicked his tail side to side, and rippled his skin, apparently asking for another rubdown. Barabbas, with great appreciation for such a gentle (when he wanted to be), indispensable animal, began to oblige.

Having clued the people in on his trek down and up the line and warning them of the long day ahead, camp was broken, gear packed, and everyone was ready to move out at first light. Mary walked for an hour, then elected to ride again. She wasn't as perky as yesterday. As her mother was fussing over her, wrapping her in warm cloaks and gloves, she gave Joseph and Barabbas an anxious look from behind Mary's back. Both men kept a cheerful countenance but each felt apprehensive about what the day might bring.

"Let's move!" Barabbas called again in his loud voice and, slapping Hiram sharply on the rump again, said gently, "Careful, donkey, careful."

Setting what he judged to be the fastest pace possible for the slowest family to maintain, Barabbas ranged out ahead a considerable distance. About an hour later a shrill whistle from Joseph stopped him, and he turned quickly. Seeing Joseph's beckoning arm wave, his heart stopped momentarily and he had to swallow to get it down out of his throat. He started back in a dead run but slowed down a bit as Joseph strode out to meet him, giving him an all-clear signal.

"Man, you scared me to death," exclaimed Barabbas. "What's up?"

"Mary wants some conversation with you. Says she has a complaint," answered Joseph.

Sounds reassuring, thought Barabbas. *A complaint can't be a major event.*

Barabbas and Joseph waited for Hiram to reach them, turned and walked alongside. "What's your complaint now?" Barabbas asked, as if this was an hourly occurrence, his smile belying the tone of voice.

"Barabbas, why are we running?" Mary asked.

"You know why we're walking fast—not running. You want to have that baby out here in a snowstorm?"

"We haven't seen a snowflake since breaking camp," Mary replied tartly, her smile easing the weight of her words. "And the faster Hiram walks, the harder his feet hit the ground. You're jostling me to pieces." Another smile. "Besides, we're all overlooking something."

"And just what have we overlooked?" Barabbas asked, a hint of tartness in his own voice, his brow furrowed in thought as he tried in vain to remember what he had failed to pack.

"Remember, about a year ago, Rabbi Bethel read from the Micah scroll? 'But you, Bethlehem Ephrathah, . . . out of you will come for me one who will be ruler over Israel, . . . from ancient times.' And so on. Don't you remember?"

"Remember a Scripture reading from a Sabbath synagogue meeting a year ago? Of course I don't. I don't know how you remember it either. What has that—"

"If you were a woman you would remember," Mary interrupted. "And I've heard my father read it too, in our home. Bet you have heard your father read it. If you would only pay attention!"

"Just what are you trying to say, woman?"

"Don't you see? This baby," patting her stomach, "is to be born in Bethlehem! We can't tempt or try to thwart God by sitting out here twiddling our thumbs, but we don't have to run either."

"You're saying then that if we take two more days to Bethlehem, instead of one, that the baby won't be born out here in this snowstorm?"

Barabbas waved his arms in a 360 degree turn around the horizon and squinted his eyes up into the sunshine above.

Mary had to laugh at his capitulation, as did Joseph.

There it is again, thought Barabbas. *This baby is the son of God, promised by God, conceived by God. Got to be born in Bethlehem. Wish I could be so sure. And it is going to snow. Look at those clouds gathering!*

He left Joseph to set a slower pace and walked back down and up the line, telling everyone they were slowing down, taking the four-day pace to their destination, due to arrive about the ninth hour. To his surprise he got several cheers and some strained smiles of appreciation.

CHAPTER FOURTEEN

The morning of the fourth day Barabbas had to fight a battle to keep from running again. Yesterday Mary had not walked a mile before she asked to be helped to her seat on Hiram, and this morning she had asked Joseph to fix her a place in the oxcart.

He began to picture Bethlehem in his mind. He had gone down there a few times while in Jerusalem, on what he called "recruiting trips." He had met Joab who ran the Red Lion Tavern and Inn on the main approach to the town from the north. After two or three visits with Joab and a lot of bantering back and forth he had felt safe enough to bring up the subject of the brigands. Joab had been interested and sympathetic with the cause, but due to the business he was in—renting rooms, selling alcoholic drinks, and catering to such a rough element—he had obliquely forestalled

Barabbas from any further discussion of the organization. Then, too, as Levi had pointed out, Bethlehem was too small to conceal an active cell.

It's too small to take care of this crowd, Barabbas thought darkly. *Some of these will drop off with relatives in Jerusalem; some will scatter out elsewhere. I'll get rooms at the Red Lion for Mary and Joseph and her folks. I can set up the tent for mine.* So the planning went on in his head, and in spite of Mary's calm assurance about the birth of her baby, Barabbas kept the caravan moving until dusky dark. The third day had been uneventful. Perhaps it was because of the slowed pace of the day before, perhaps because of a good night's sleep. At any rate, Mary was big, slow, and somewhat clumsy but inordinately cheerful as they moved out on this fourth day. She chose to ride the cart again. As Joseph was arranging things to make her as comfortable as possible, she spoke up brightly, "We'll be in Bethlehem tonight."

Joseph's heart dropped to his shoes. Before they had left Nazareth, in answer to Barabbas's question, "When?" Mary had answered, "Anytime." Second day out, in order to slow Barabbas down, she had assured them the baby was to be born in Bethlehem. This morning it's "Tonight we'll be in Bethlehem!"

Joseph settled his mother in with Mary, placed his father at the side of the ox with the goad in his hand, and set out to find Barabbas.

The caravan was moving the same pace as the last two days when Barabbas strode up front, having finished his checkup of the caravanners down the line and back. He could sense Joseph's agitation before he reached him.

"Everything all right this morning?" he asked.

"Did you stop and talk to Mary?" Joseph's tone implied: "If you didn't, you should've."

Barabbas answered, "No. She and your mother were in an earnest conversation, and I didn't think I ought to interrupt. What's eating on you?"

"We'll be in Bethlehem tonight."

"So what? We thought when we left Nazareth it would take four days. Could have done it in three if she hadn't said the baby had to be born in . . ." Barabbas stopped, clicked his jaws shut, and looked keenly at Joseph. "What happened this morning?"

Joseph told Barabbas how well things had gone: Mary bright and cheerful, helping her mother around the cook fire while he and his father took care of the stock, struck the tent, loaded everything, so on and so on. Then, "When I was fixing her place in the cart she looks up and says 'We'll be in Bethlehem tonight.'" Barabbas opened his mouth to reply when Joseph continued, "I know. She just made a statement. But Barabbas, it was how she said it and how she looked when she said it. Sounded sort of . . ." Joseph looked for a word and said, "final—like this is what I was chosen to do. It's . . . My time is up. Gabriel said I was to bear God's son. I told him it would be as he said. Barabbas, I could read all that in her face and in her voice. Tonight, if we reach Bethlehem, her baby will be born."

Barabbas had a sinking feeling in his stomach, such as Joseph had that morning. Hearing the desperation in Joseph's voice he reached the same conclusion. He had tended enough sheep to know that the mother ewe sensed when her time had come and instinctively went to what she considered an appropriate place to give birth.

Barabbas took a deep breath. This wasn't a sheep they were talking about. This was Mary—and Joseph.

I've got to calm this man down, he thought.

Walking along in step with Joseph, Barabbas put his arm around Joseph's shoulders.

"Well, it's not like we didn't know this was going to happen. We've known since early spring. So let's not be surprised and panic." He scanned the sky briefly. "It's coming on to snow again. Go on back and walk with your father. You can rig a canvas shelter for them when it starts. We'll sight Jerusalem about midafternoon. Some of these people will drop out there. When they do, come up here and lead for me. Bethlehem is about six more miles, and I'll want to run ahead and pin down a couple or three rooms at an inn I know."

Barabbas's calm voice and his assessment of the situation, plus his apparent control had the desired effect.

"Right," Joseph replied. "I'll take care of things back there and be back up here later. We'll have our usual nooning?"

"Yeah. We have to eat, and the stock has to be cared for. You'll be busy."

Barabbas smiled at Joseph and gave him a gentle push on his way.

The nooning was not exactly routine. It had turned much colder and, while the animals were fed and watered, the people did not fare so well. The wind was up, the snow was falling, and since they were nearing their destination, most chose to do without cook fires and made do with leftovers. This made for some whining children, but they finally filled up on fruit and nuts and were satisfied with the promise of a hot meal for supper. Barabbas made his usual check down and back up the line and received many thank-yous and smiles of appreciation for his care, interest, and leadership. He checked on his parents, saw that Joseph had adequately cared for Mary and his mother, and they both made their way up front.

Since the weather was worsening, Barabbas thought it expedient that he step up the pace a bit. He was pleased but not surprised that there were no objections. Everyone seemed anxious and ready to end the arduous journey.

Don't blame 'em, thought Barabbas. *I'll be glad when this night's over!*

He was pleased that the snow was somewhat intermittent again. If it had continued as it was at the noon stop, the accumulation under foot could become a problem. Barabbas kept up the pace, and when the skyline of Jerusalem finally came into view, he was much nearer the city than he had anticipated. Veering off to the west, he led out on the road less traveled, which would bypass Jerusalem and lead to Bethlehem. Looking back, he saw that the caravan began to split into two: His parents, Joseph with Mary, and their parents were taking the Bethlehem road, followed at intervals by other families. But the main body was on the main road to Jerusalem. As he continued to look back he was interested in seeing the widening develop, the short leg following him and the longer leg stretching almost to the gates of Jerusalem.

It wasn't long before Joseph came jogging up.

"Everyone is bearing up but looking forward to a warm room and a hot meal. When should we get there?" he asked.

"About an hour, maybe two. I'll run on and make ready. There are some people on the road ahead of us. I'll get there well before they do. You'll see the Red Lion Tavern right on the road. I'll be there waiting for you." He grinned at Joseph, "I don't suppose we need to worry about Mary until she sets foot in Bethlehem."

"Get on with you," said Joseph. "I'm worried already. We may be close enough!"

The men embraced, Barabbas turned and began to run.

About an hour later Barabbas pulled up in front of the Red Lion, a look of confused wonder on his face. It had begun to snow again. Not the cold, blowing frenzy of the noon stop, but softly falling flakes wafting gently to the ground, beginning to cover with a clean white blanket the clutter and mess around the courtyard and under the windows of the Red Lion. It was also muffling the sound of passing travelers on the roadway, both voices and hoofbeats. But nothing could muffle the sound of the yells, curses, loud music and unholy din emanating from within the Red Lion. With a sinking feeling to his very bones, he knew he couldn't subject Mary and Joseph, their parents and his, to any such conditions. Not knowing what else to do, he took a tentative step toward the courtyard of the Red Lion when he heard, "Barabbas?"

Startled at hearing his name, he turned and looked. Standing out at the edge of the roadway stood a dim figure in the gloom, one hand shading his eyes from the snow, the other arm raised in a sort of greeting.

"Yes?" wiping the snow from his face and shading his own eyes, Barabbas moved cautiously toward the man.

"It's me, Judas." Barabbas could hear the relief in his voice.

"Glory to God, boy! Am I glad to see you!" Barabbas took Judas in such a bear hug it swept him off his feet and took his breath. But he was shyly pleased with his reception.

He had not known Barabbas very long but had enjoyed working with him in the shop and openly idolized him for his physical prowess, exuberance, and sense of humor.

"What am I going to do about this mess?" Barabbas asked, putting the boy back down on his feet and pointing at the Red Lion with his chin. Barabbas was not much older than Judas in years, but right now he felt like an old, old man. And he wondered why an old, old man would be asking a mere lad for advice in such a predicament as he now found himself.

"We are to go inside for a minute or so, and see Joab," replied Judas. Taking Barabbas by the arm and walking through the courtyard to the door of the Red Lion, Barabbas permitted himself to be led, turning over in his mind what Judas had said: "We are to go . . ." as if he were obeying orders.

As they opened the door and stepped inside, such a blast of stale hot air, odious smell, vulgar language, and licentious behavior assailed his senses that he tried to hold his breath.

"What in the name of God is going on?" Barabbas muttered under his breath. Judas heard him in spite of the din.

"Nothing's going on in the name of God," Judas replied. "Well, maybe it is. Joab has tried to clean the place out, but the soldiers came and—here he comes now. He can tell you."

Joab walked up, carrying a good-sized club, smiled weakly at Barabbas, took him by the arm, and led him and Judas back out into the courtyard.

"My friend, I'm glad to see you. Reuben told me you would be in today. Whew! It's good to get out of that stench for a few minutes."

"What has happened to your place?" Barabbas demanded. "Have you turned it over to the devil and his legions?"

"Looks like it, doesn't it?" said Joab. "But it's a long story, and I've got to get back inside. Briefly, the riffraff came to Bethlehem soon after the notices went up. They smelled money and pleasure—women. They decided to make the Red Lion their headquarters. Things began to get out of hand in a couple of weeks, and I went out, enlisted a group of my kind of riffraff, and was going to throw them out.

"A captain of Caesar's legions got word of my plans, came to see me, and offered me a deal. It seems they would prefer to keep this crowd more or less bottled up out here on the outskirts than to have them loose on the streets of the town. The legions hassle me once in a while—fighting, disorderly conduct, and so on. He said if I kept 'em out here, they would try to return the favor after the census is over. He has even given me two men around the clock, out of uniform of course, to help keep order. And he leads a company of men by at odd hours, day and night, in a show of strength and authority. It's the best I could do."

"I see," responded Barabbas. "You're over a barrel. But my crowd's due in here in about an hour. What am I going to do with 'em?"

"Hasn't Judas told you? About the stable?" A crash and a tinkle of pottery caught his attention. "I've got to go. I think you're taken care of." The last remark came from over his shoulder as he took a firm grip on his club and disappeared through the door.

CHAPTER FIFTEEN

arabbas looked at Judas.

"Start talking, boy. What's this about a stable? And why are you here in Bethlehem instead of Jerusalem making tents? And what am I going to do with the folks off that caravan? Boy, we've got to do something."

Judas took Barabbas by the arm again.

"Come on this way, 'round back and up the hill a ways. Has that lady had her baby yet?"

Barabbas's abrupt stop and jerk broke Judas's grip on his arm.

"Boy, you're confusing me! Have I got to get a club and beat some information out of you! What do you know about a lady having a baby?"

Judas did not take Barabbas by the arm again. He motioned with his head and started walking again.

"I've heard you and Reuben talk about her while we're working in the shop."

Barabbas caught up with Judas and took him by the arm.

Judas continued, "And Reuben said yesterday it may be born already."

"Reuben was here yesterday?"

"Yeah," answered Judas. "We came to Bethlehem day before yesterday. Reuben said you had been to the Red Lion and would likely be figuring to put up there. Like you, he wanted to check it out when he heard all that commotion."

Judas grinned slyly at Barabbas. "He wouldn't let me go in. Said I was too young."

"You foxed me, didn't you?" growled Barabbas. "Go on."

"He talked with Joab and got the same story you got. And Joab told us to go see the stable. Sent his oldest boy with us to show the way. He's my age, and he stays in the Red Lion." Judas sounded a bit resentful.

"Don't you worry about Joab's oldest boy. You may be the same age, but in his case, age don't count. Go on."

Barabbas saw the flickering light of a fire from around the hill on his right. "Here's the stock pen," said Judas. "The animals usually stay in the stable, a cave cut in the hillside, but when Joab's wife came out and saw what we had done here, she said this was all right. See, we hung canvas around two sides for a windbreak and rigged a canvas shelter to keep 'em dry. The cave is this way."

Judas led Barabbas around a huge outcropping of rock, and there, with double wooden doors propped open and a fire burning to one side, was the cave-stable, about fifteen feet wide and twenty feet deep.

Judas continued, "Don't know how long it's been since it's been cleaned out. Reuben, me and Jesse—that's Joab's boy—worked all day yesterday and put the canvas down this morning. Still smells like a stable, but it's clean. Joab's wife, her name is Ruth, said she was going to have Jesse or somebody to clean it everyday when they start putting the stock back in here. Go on in and take a look."

Judas gave the invitation to "take a look" with pride in his voice. Barabbas went in with some trepidation and was thunderstruck with what must have been a major and miraculous transformation. The walls and ceiling showed signs of having been swept down with brush brooms. No cobwebs, no loose dirt likely to fall. He couldn't see the floor; about two thirds of it was covered with canvas and fresh straw. Four oil lamps on brackets imbedded in the walls lit about a third of the front area and two unlit lamps were on the back wall.

Barabbas walked slowly around the interior in a daze, reaching out at intervals to touch the walls in disbelief. Judas watched with some anxiety. Barabbas walked back to the entrance and felt the warmth of the fire on his face. He stepped outside, stopped still, and listened intently. The only sound he heard was the silent whisper of falling snowflakes and the comforting snuffling of the animals nearby. Turning, he walked back inside and took a long look around again, not walking, just turning his head.

"Judas," he whispered softly. "It's a palace."

A pleased look spread over Judas's face. For him, this was high praise from a big, strapping man who had recently become an idol to a still growing boy.

"So," said Barabbas, "let's get back on the road in front of the Red Lion. The folks should be here soon. By the way, what about Reuben? When is he coming back?"

"He wanted to be at the shop when his folks showed up. Has a place for them in one of Levi's buildings. He didn't say when he would be back. You go on back to the Red Lion. I'll stay here, stoke up the fire, and bring up some more wood. These folks are going to be cold and hungry."

"Right you are, boy—I mean, *man*. You've grown up since I left Jerusalem and went home. I can't call you boy anymore." Barabbas hesitated a moment. Then, "But you still can't go in the Red Lion!"

Judas grinned and turned to the fire while Barabbas made his way back to the inn.

He took his place in the courtyard so he could watch the road and had not been there more than ten minutes when he heard a familiar *clop, clop, clop* of donkey hooves. Barabbas felt he would recognize those footsteps if he went to sleep and woke up in the middle of the Egyptian desert. He strode quickly out into the road and called out, not too loudly, "Yo, Hiram!"

He knew the response he would get before it came, a bray that would have rattled the doors and windows of any building in Bethlehem other than the Red Lion. And it was followed immediately by a shout he also recognized, his father's. He and Hiram both appeared out of the gloom, and in the distance, somewhat muffled by the snow, he heard the creaking, squeaking rattle of wheels, harness, and other accouterments of a mobile people.

Hiram came up, ears laid back and tail switching, and pushed his head gently against Barabbas's stomach. Patting his neck and pulling his ears, Barabbas peered into the dark of night as his father appeared, out of breath from trying to keep up with Hiram.

"Where's Joseph?" Barabbas asked. "Did they have to stop?"

"No. They're next in line, but it's going to be a near thing," his father gasped. "I've seen often enough your mama go through this. Mary wanted her mama in the cart and Joseph walking 'longside. So Hiram led out, and I tried to keep up. Here they come. Where are we going? Not in there!" pointing toward the Red Lion and making a statement.

"No, not in there," Barabbas answered. "Wait for them. Watch where I'm going and follow me and Hiram's tracks. In a minute or two you'll see the light of a fire. That's the place."

Barabbas and Hiram approached the fire and Judas looked up expectantly.

"Are they here yet?" he asked.

"About ten, fifteen minutes," Barabbas replied. "Rake some coals out to one side so Mama can put on a stew pot. They'll be hungry, and she'll want to start cooking the minute she gets here."

"Right," Judas replied, "then I'll go put the donkey in the pen. Is this the Hiram I've been hearing about?"

"Yes, it is," answered Barabbas, looking balefully at Hiram, "and you can't."

"Can't what?" asked Judas. He stopped raking coals and looked at Barabbas.

"You can't put him in the pen," snorted Barabbas. "He won't go."

Judas looked at Hiram, back at Barabbas, then started raking coals again.

"And just why won't he?" he asked. Like Barabbas might be soft in the head.

"Because he knows Mary won't be in the pen, that's why." Still glaring at Hiram, "I have the idea he's going to stay close to her."

"In the cave?!" shouted Judas, dropping his scoop and jumping to his feet. "He can't do that! We just got that place cleaned out."

Now Judas was glaring at both Hiram and Barabbas. Hiram wasn't looking at anybody. He was asleep on his feet again.

The sound of the approaching travelers ended the discussion, except for Hiram. He looked up, laid back his ears, and brayed a welcome.

A babble of conversation erupted. "Where's the stew pot? Where are we? In a *stable*—in a cave? Oh no! She's in labor! This baby will not be born in a stable! I have never . . . Where's the rest of that lamb I was cooking? Joseph, did you hear what—? Don't tell Mary that . . ."

A shrill whistle cut the air like a knife. All of a sudden, silence.

"All right," Barabbas spoke with a voice of authority. "We could not stay in the inn. No room. It has been taken over by drunks, harlots, scoundrels—you name it, it's in there. We couldn't stay in there even if they had rooms.

"Reuben and Judas here," putting his arm around Judas's shoulders, "came over from Jerusalem two, three days ago and, with the help of the innkeeper's son, they cleaned out and dressed up the stable. It smells a little," Barabbas admitted, grudgingly, "but it's a lot more desirable than the inn. Joseph, you and Mary's parents take her inside. Judas, run in and light the other lamps. It's Mary's baby. I think she and Joseph will like the place. I see Mama's got the pot on. Just be quiet until we have inspection."

About ten minutes later Mary appeared in the doorway, supported on each side by Joseph and her mother. She was in obvious pain, but the expression on her face was beautiful.

"It's perfect," she said, "fit for a king. Thank you, old friend," looking at Barabbas. "And thank you, new friend," looking at Judas. The simple words, tone, and dazzling smile she gave him bound this young lad forever to the life and fortunes of this mother-to-be in such a way that he never forgot this moment.

"Now, Mama, if you'll fix my bed, I think I had better lie down." Turning, Mama and Joseph led her back inside.

In a moment, Joseph appeared in the doorway and approached the fire.

"I was invited outside and ordered not to return until called for," he announced to all present. "Furthermore, I was asked to unload the cart of all Mary's things, put them in the doorway, and was told," to Barabbas's mother, "that you would bring them inside."

"You boys finish this cooking, make some bread, and we will let you know when to bring it to the door. And," rather tartly, "seems to me you might rig a shelter, put up a tent. You're going to be out here all night!"

Joseph went to the stew pot; his father began making the bread; his mother took a jar of water into the cave; and Barabbas, his father, and Judas put up the tent, rolling up the side nearest the fire. With the tent up and secure, Barabbas went over to help Joseph and his father with the cooking.

When did this labor business start?" he asked. "Was she scared?"

"About midafternoon—and no, she wasn't scared. At least, not for the baby." Joseph looked around to see if anyone was within earshot. "She said the baby wouldn't come until we got here. She was positive about that, and she also said the baby would be perfect: ten fingers and ten toes." Joseph smiled briefly, looking around again. "You know what she meant? It's God's baby. Can't be anything but perfect. But Barabbas, she said something else. Scared me. She said the baby had to be perfect, but Gabriel hadn't promised her a thing! Do you think she might die? What would I do with a newborn baby?"

Barabbas shook his head, "I haven't known what to think about all this." He was thinking to himself, *If I had been talking to Gabriel, whoever he is, I would have found out more about her role in what's going on.* But he bit his tongue!

Joseph continued; "I got the impression she's thinking that with the birth of this baby, that may be all God wants of her—she might just die. I can't believe the God we know would do that. Do you?"

"No, I don't think He would do that. Look at all the babies old folks have had—Isaac, Samuel. Hey, how about baby John being born to Elizabeth? God is merciful, Joseph, to those who love and serve Him." He said this, listening all the while to the moans and groans coming through the one open door to the stable. Joseph, busy over the cook fire and farther away, couldn't hear this. *Good thing, too,* thought Barabbas. *Wish I couldn't.*

The fathers of Barabbas, Joseph, and Mary, knowing how useless and unnecessary men were in this situation, saw that the food was ready and proceeded to eat. Judas, Barabbas, and Joseph, realizing how hungry they were, decided now was the time to do likewise. Barabbas purposely moved as far away as he could get from the stable entrance, motioning for Joseph to follow him.

"Barabbas?"

Hearing the question in Judas's voice, Barabbas looked at him. Judas pointed his chin toward the stable door. Barabbas looked. There, all he saw was Hiram's rear quarters. Head, neck, and shoulders were inside.

Muttering under his breath, Barabbas put his dish aside, rose to his feet, and started around the fire toward the doorway. As he drew near, Hiram moved completely inside, out of sight.

Stooping slightly, Barabbas called out, "Send that dumb brute out here!"

"He's not a dumb brute, I told you." It was Mary, gasping. "I told him to come in."

His mother added, "We'll put him in the back. We've already doused the lamps back there. If it looks like he has to go, we'll send him out." Mary giggled between gasps. Barabbas smiled.

He walked back around the fire, sat down, and picked up his plate.

"Don't think you need to worry about Mary," he stated. "I heard her laugh."

Joseph loosened up a bit. Judas didn't.

"If that jackass messes up that cave, I'll take a club to him," he muttered.

"Just don't let him hear you call him a jackass," said Barabbas. "Or Mary either for that matter." Both men laughed and loosened up a little more. Judas wasn't having any of it. He was over at the woodpile, talking under his breath, looking for a club.

CHAPTER
SIXTEEN

About an hour later Mary's mother hurried out the doorway and over to the cart, tossing things about until, apparently finding what she was looking for, grabbed it up and bustled back into the stable. Almost instantly the men heard the faint cry and whimper of a baby, which immediately turned into more lusty sounds of protest. There were also louder sounds of approbation from all the mamas in attendance.

Joseph and Barabbas were getting to their feet when Joseph's mother came to the door. "Joseph, you've got a fine boy in here. I think maybe you can hear him. Empty this basin, put some hot water in it, and cool it down a bit with some clean snow."

"How about Mary?" he asked anxiously. "How is she?"

"Fine. Just fine. Wrung out, but all right. Hurry now."

While Joseph stood there in a trance, Barabbas took the basin from his hands, walked out some distance, and emptied it on the ground. Going back to the cook fire, he ladled in some hot water, swirling it around in the basin as he walked back to the same spot and emptied it again. Going back by the tent, he raked some snow off the top into the basin. Then went by the fire and ladled more hot water. The rising steam warmed his face and hands as he took the basin to the stable door.

"You aiming to stand here all night?" he asked the still-transfixed Joseph. "Here, see if they'll let you in with this basin of water."

Joseph came to with a start, looking at both Barabbas and the basin as if he had never before seen either one. Taking the basin he turned and walked slowly inside.

Hope he gets there with it, thought Barabbas, grinning at the mental image of a twenty-seven year-old, first-class, accomplished carpenter and woodworker in such a state of helplessness.

"Is the baby here? Is that beautiful lady all right?" asked Judas anxiously.

"Yes, to both questions, I would say," said Barabbas. "Let's get our dishes cleaned up and ready to serve the women. They don't know it now, but in about half an hour they'll think they're starving to death."

CHAPTER
SEVENTEEN

As Judas washed and dried the dishes, Barabbas filled them with food. Taking a plate and a basket of freshly made bread, he went to the stable door and asked, "Anyone in here hungry?" A chorus of "yeah" and "starving" was flung back at him. Returning toward the fire from delivering the last plate, Barabbas was somewhat startled to hear a babble of voices coming from the fields and pasturelands in the direction opposite the way to the Red Lion. Looking that way, he could see that one or two people were carrying torches to light the way.

"Pssst! Look alive! Get your staffs!" he whispered loudly.

The men scrambled to their feet from under the shelter, each with staff in hand. Judas, not having a staff, grabbed the club he had selected for Hiram and turned in the direction in which Barabbas was looking. As the light from the fire illumined his face and figure, they heard, "Hey, Judas? That you?"

Judas wiped the snowflakes from his face and peered into the swirling darkness.

"It's Daniel." To Barabbas, "Joab's second oldest," he explained. "He's out with the sheep.

"Yeah, Daniel," he called loudly. "Come on in."

Judas unobtrusively laid aside his club and with hand signals, indicated that the others do the same.

"We just saw and heard the strangest thing; none of us can believe it happened," Daniel said, wonder in his voice. "These two were with me and them three," pointing, "were about a mile away. The other three," pointing again, "were out in another direction. We all saw and heard the same thing."

"Saw and heard what?" Barabbas asked.

All started talking at once, each trying to be heard above the other.

Barabbas's whistle cut the air again, stopping all conversation immediately.

"You," he pointed to the one he took to be the oldest. "What did you see? And hear," he added.

"A great light," the man blurted. "Bright as day! I could see every sheep, every dog, every bush and stone." There was awe and wonder on his face and in his voice.

"And you?" Barabbas asked, pointing to one who was in another group Daniel had indicated.

"Angels," said this one. "Angels everywhere. Flying all over. Whirling, dipping, soaring. Like swallows over a grain field. And music like you never heard. Instruments and singing. I recognized some of the songs of David. I was scared out of my wits, but it was beautiful."

"Did you see the light, too?" Barabbas asked.

"Oh, yes," was the reply. "Look up. You can't see the moon, not a star. But out there it was like you could see forever!"

"How about you?" Barabbas asked, looking at Daniel.

"It's as the others have said," Daniel answered. "We three saw the same things." He looked at the other two for corroboration. They nodded solemnly. "And heard the same things. Angels flying, playing harps, and singing, 'Glory to God in the Highest! Don't be afraid. I bring you good news.'" He looked again at his two companions, then at the other six. All nodded in agreement. "One said that today, in the City of David, a Savior has been born who is Christ the Lord. We're going into Bethlehem to see this baby we were told about."

Barabbas opened his mouth to speak when Judas, eyes and voice filled with wonder, blurted out, "A beautiful lady just had a baby." To Daniel, "Here in your stable, not more than an hour ago. A boy baby, would you like to see him?"

A chorus: "Oh yes. Of course we would. Indeed we would. We all met out in the pastures and agreed we had to go in to Bethlehem to see what has come to pass. We left the sheep. But we feel sure they are safe. He's in Joab's stable?"

Barabbas, hearing this last remark, noted with wonder that there was no surprise, no doubt, no confusion, as if a baby being born in a stable was an everyday occurrence. *So be it,* he thought.

He went to the stable entrance, opened the other double door that had remained closed, and stepped inside. The women and Joseph looked up expectantly.

"You've come to see the baby?" asked Mary, her voice strong and vibrant.

"My father, two grandfathers, and Judas are outside, and they want to see the baby. There are nine, I said nine shepherds outside and they want to see the baby. They were in groups of three, scattered all over the landscape. They all saw and heard the same things: A bright light shone all around; angels flew all about, playing instruments, singing and praising God. They were told about the birth of a baby in Bethlehem, and they've come to see him. All right?"

Again, Barabbas was amazed that no one seemed to think it was unusual, a singular event, for nine shepherds to show up from out of nowhere, to see a newborn baby.

"Where is he?" he asked, looking around, puzzled.

"Over there in the manger," answered Mary's mother. "Yes, bring them on in."

Barabbas stepped outside. "The women are pleased that you have come to see the baby, but," to the shepherds, "do you mind if my father and the two grandfathers go in first? They haven't see him yet."

"Oh, no," responded the older shepherd who had spoken first about what they had seen. "Grandfathers are special. Let them go first."

The men crowded in, quietly and silently, and the grandfathers and Barabbas's father were led by Mary's mother over to the manger.

"This is Joseph, the proud father," said Barabbas, "and the girl whose hand he's holding is the new mother," he continued.

"We are so glad you've come," Mary said warmly. "He's sleeping, but you can see he's a very handsome—no, a very beautiful baby."

The grandfathers moved away, and the shepherds gathered around the manger, looking with wonder, awe, and reverence at this small child whose arrival had been proclaimed in such a spectacular manner. It *was* a pretty child, a baby like all other babies they had ever seen. The father and mother, handsome and pretty, looked like most other parents they all had seen. *In fact*, thought the older man who seemed to be spokesman for the group, *they are not unlike me and my wife. And our babies were no different from this one—in appearance. But there has to be something special.* He looked over at Mary and spoke softly, "Ma'am, may I touch him?"

"Of course," answered Mary. "If you like, Grandma here," looking at her mother, "will pick him up and let you hold him."

"No, no, that won't be needful. Just a touch." Leaning over the manger, he gently placed his big, calloused hand on the baby's head, covering it completely. He was not a prayerful man, but he thought to himself, *Jehovah, bless and keep safe this little one.* The little one stirred under his hand, and he raised it quickly lest he wake him. Looking down on the child once more, he turned and led the others away. Stopping by Mary and Joseph again he said, "Thank you, sir, ma'am. What's the child's name?"

"He is to be called Jesus," she answered. "And thank you. I know you prayed for him."

The shepherd repeated, in a whisper, "Jesus, Jesus, Jesus," smiled at Mary again, and slowly preceded the others out the door.

CHAPTER
EIGHTEEN

No one broke the silence that ensued after the exit of the shepherds. Each seemed lost in his or her own deep thoughts, filled with wonder at what they had just heard. Only Mary, Joseph, and Barabbas knew of the visit and words of Gabriel. Only they could put two and two together and accept as fact what the shepherds had said.

The others knew about dreams, visions. They all at some time or other had dreamed strange dreams; in deep, sometimes troubled, sleep had seen strange sights. Surely this is what had happened with the shepherds. Each thought in his and her own mind, *This is too unbelievable. That is just a newborn Jewish boy, born to an ordinary Jewish girl and her ordinary Jewish husband. Who in Nazareth, or anywhere else for that matter, would believe a story about bright lights, angels flying all over, singing, and playing instruments? I'm not about to go back home and tell any such story.*

On impulse, Mary's mother was the first to move. She rose to her feet, walked over to the manger, and stared down at the child. Seeing nothing unusual she drew back the blanket that covered him. As Mary had said, "Ten fingers and ten toes!" Covering him again, she turned, looked at the others, shook her head slightly, and began to clean up the supper dishes.

At this, the other women began to do the things that needed to be done. The men looked at each other and moved toward the doorway. All except Judas. He removed a lamp from its bracket, went to the back of the cave, and made a quick but thorough inspection. Finding nothing amiss, he gave Hiram a warning look, replaced the lamp, and went outside.

"But Mary treasured up all these things and pondered them in her heart," wondering what the future held for her and this baby asleep on the hay in a manger. Of one thing she was certain: The shepherds had seen what they said they had seen. Like the older women in the stable with her, whose reasoning they did not express but which she saw and understood, neither could she talk about lights, angels, singing, and musical instruments. She, Joseph, and Barabbas could discuss it among themselves but with no one else.

Mary was determined that no stigma of speculation, gossip, questions, or raised eyebrows would revolve around this baby of hers. He was a Jewish boy baby, due to circumstances beyond anyone's control, born in a stable in Bethlehem. He would be reared like other Jewish males. God willing—she smiled—he would have brothers and sisters. They would be no different from any other family in Nazareth. She smiled happily and drifted off to sleep.

CHAPTER NINETEEN

Outside the snow had ceased, but it was still cold. It had been a long day and all were tired. Joseph stoked the fire, and Barabbas went to the pen to check on the animals. The older men stood at the fire, warming their backsides, and soon hurried into the tent and to bed. Barabbas came back into the firelight, saw Judas sitting next to Joseph, his chin buried in his chest, sound asleep. Shaking him gently, Judas jerked awake. Barabbas smiled at him, nodded toward the tent, and with no protest whatever, Judas rose and stumbled blindly into the tent.

Barabbas and Joseph continued to sit by the fire, replenishing it at intervals, each lost in his own thoughts. Finally, "Well, Barabbas, what do you think?"

"I think we had better forget the whole thing," answered Barabbas.

"Can't very well forget a baby has been born!" Joseph grinned at him.

"You know what I mean," Barabbas said. "Let's forget the shepherds. They will tell their story to anybody who'll listen. Some few will hear and wonder. Most will hear and laugh, 'Drunk! Asleep and dreaming.' When the shepherds see and hear that reaction, they'll slow down. If none of us talk about it, when everybody gets registered and goes back home, I think the story will die. . . . Except for the older fellow who asked to touch him."

"And asked his name," added Joseph.

"Yeah," conceded Barabbas, "He'll remember. . . . But I don't think he will be broadcasting this story. I think he sees what you and Mary know, that somehow and for some reason this child is special, unusual, destined for great things. As I said, I don't think he'll say so. If he keeps quiet, if we," waving his hand around to include everyone from Nazareth, "keep quiet, what talking the shepherds do can't matter too much."

"Barabbas?"

"Yeah?"

"You said this older fellow sees what I and Mary know. What do you know, or why don't you believe?"

"Good question," answered Barabbas. "And I can't answer it. I don't know why I don't believe like you and Mary do. Maybe it's because you two talked to Gabriel and I didn't. Joseph, I've tried. I just can't do it."

A long pause. Then, "Barabbas?"

"Yeah?"

"Do you think the baby's mine?"

"Good God Almighty, no!" Barabbas almost shouted. "That I do know. Joseph, the trouble is in me, not between

us. Give me time. I've a feeling it'll work out. May take years,"
a rueful smile, "but don't give up on me. Next to my parents,
you and Mary, and now Jesus, are the best I've got. Overlook
my faults. Be patient."

"You've got all the time it takes, friend. I'm not sleepy—
too much on my mind—but I think I'll stretch out here by
the fire. Are you going inside?"

"No, I'll stay out here. Want to keep the fire going. Go to
sleep. I'm used to busy nights."

"Yeah, I know. We worry about that too."

Joseph was soon asleep, and Barabbas was left alone with
his thoughts.

Several times during the night he heard some stirring
around in the stable, and once or twice heard the baby cry,
then the soothing voice of his mother, singing a soft little
sleepy song.

About the sixth hour he heard a noise, looked up, and
watched Hiram walk quietly through the door. He walked
out a short distance, snuffled and blew out a long breath,
shook himself until his ears flapped, then disappeared. Some
time later he heard him at the outside food trough.

That's one smart jackass, thought Barabbas, grinning. *Judas will be pleased to know.*

Oddly enough, Hiram did not return to the stable. Stoking the fire to a brighter light, Barabbas went toward the
stock pen for a better look. Hiram was lying as close as he
could get to Joseph's ox, which was lying inside the pen. Shaking his head in puzzlement, he walked back to the fire.

I don't understand donkeys either, he thought.

CHAPTER TWENTY

By the ninth hour Barabbas had breakfast ready. Everyone began to stir, and Reuben showed up with an appetite. He and Barabbas hugged, thumped, and danced each other around in a boyish show of exuberant affection. Mary recognizing his voice called for him to come in, where he was greeted effusively. Paying his proper respects to all and waxing eloquent about the baby, he came back outside to go through somewhat the same ceremony with the men. Finally, they settled down to eat while Judas insisted on ferrying the food inside to the women. Just as Barabbas thought he had better put on another pot and make some more bread, eating slowed to a halt and conversation began.

The main topic of conversation was the registration. How long do you suppose it will take? About how many people are in town? Some are in Jerusalem; they'll have to come over here. How many registration places are there? Most everyone had an opinion, but no one knew anything. After all, they just got here last night.

To bring some order out of chaos, Barabbas suggested that his father and the two grandfathers go into town and get some answers. Seeing some way to be and feel useful they quickly agreed, and with explanations to their wives, off they went.

Barabbas, Reuben, and Judas cleaned up the pots and dishes. His mother came out, thanked them for the two meals Barabbas and others had prepared and served, and assured him that the women were now ready to take over. Barabbas grinned and welcomed the idea.

Judas went over to water the stock, and Barabbas and Reuben each began to catch up on what the other had been doing when Judas came running back, eyes twinkling.

"What?" asked Barabbas.

"Didn't you say you tried to put Hiram in the pen and he wouldn't go?"

"That's what I said. Why?"

"Are you sure? I opened the gate and he trotted in. Looks like that's where he wanted to be all the time."

"It was like trying to move a block of temple granite," said Barabbas. "Of course, I'm sure. That dumb animal—"

"He's not dumb," said Judas. "You said yourself he came out of the stable this morning and went out yonder," pointing with his chin, "to relieve himself. I even went out to look, and found it, way, way out. He's smart. I'm going to finish watering 'em and take 'em out to pasture, and," he said over his shoulder as he jogged away, "you can burn my club!"

As Barabbas looked at the boy's retreating back, his jaw hanging, Reuben roared. Barabbas closed his mouth and gave him a feeble grin.

Wiping his eyes on his sleeve, Reuben chuckled again and resumed his questioning. "My folks said it was a pretty hard trip. Did you have any trouble?"

"Not a bit. Cold and snow, but everybody was well prepared."

"Mama said it was near thing with Mary."

Barabbas nodded his head. "Skin of our teeth. Baby was here two hours after they arrived. Pretty fast for the first one. Man, was I glad to see that fire and stable. I can never thank you enough for that."

"Seth came over here on a delivery last week," explained Reuben, "and said the town was filling up. Thought I had better check with Joab. He was already swamped. Just happened that a fellow from Capernaum showed up, a tentmaker, and asked Levi about a temporary job. Levi sent him to me. He's one of us, and I hired him on the spot. That freed me up to bring Judas over here and get the stable cleaned up. Joab's boy was a big help."

"I'll take care of him," said Barabbas. "Still busy in the shop?"

"Busy as bees. Be glad when you get back. Next week?"

"Yeah, I would guess. All those people were anxious to make a trip. Now they've made it." A pause. "I think now they want to get signed up and go home."

Reuben nodded. "Most of the pleasure in a trip is in planning and anticipation. People are funny."

So the conversation went, animated at times, idly at times, until late afternoon when the men returned. They had covered the town, talked with scores of people, and were full of information.

The women had supper about ready when the men returned and soon called everyone in. As soon as all were served and began eating, the men began to report on what they had learned during the day.

The registration was well organized and would be done in three days. It would start on the first day of the week, today being the fifth day. As soon as you registered you were free to leave and return home. As this discussion went on and on, Joseph became aware that Mary had remained silent, contemplative during all this.

"Something bothering little new mother?" he asked anxiously. "You feel all right?"

"Oh yes," she answered quickly. "I feel fine. Even helped a little bit with supper. I was just sitting here counting days—and thinking."

"What do you mean 'counting days?' And thinking what?" asked her mother.

"Well," she replied, "Jesus was born on Wednesday, fourth day of the week. Although," she smiled, "he almost made it to Thursday. That means, to be circumcised on the eighth day, next Thursday, we would be on the way home. I don't want this done on the way home. I would like for it to be done in the temple in Jerusalem."

Parents, grandparents, Barabbas, Judas, and Reuben looked at each other, mulled it over, and nodded in assent. Yet the prospect of registering and getting on the trek back to Nazareth still seemed attractive.

Mary continued, looking at Joseph, "And when the time of our purification is over, according to the Law of Moses, the firstborn son is to be presented to the Lord. I want that done in the temple in Jerusalem."

As the discussion started anew, Joseph and Barabbas looked at each other and grinned. They knew from the tone of her voice and the set of her jaw that these two "I wants" brooked no arguments. So they just sat quiet, ate their supper, and listened.

At the end of discussion the matters were settled. Everyone would register as soon as possible, according to the procedures in place. When all had done so, the older people would join whatever group was available and start toward home. Mary and Joseph would stay on in Bethlehem and take Jesus the six or seven miles to Jerusalem for his circumcision and then for his dedication. They could stay on in the stable until the influx of registrants and hangers-on cleared out, then more satisfactory arrangements could be made.

The supper dishes were cleaned up and put away, and the men took to the outside. Barabbas and Judas took care of the animals, and soon all were sleeping. Barabbas and Joseph chose to sleep outside again, knowing that one or the other would be getting up during the night to replenish the fire.

On Friday, Reuben left immediately after breakfast, returning to Jerusalem to make arrangements to bring his and other Nazareth people to Bethlehem for the registration on the first day of the week. The older women, except for Mary's mother, decided to check out Bethlehem, as the men had done the day before. Barabbas and Joseph checked with Joab to see if Mary and Joseph could continue the use of the stable for a few more days. Judas took the stock out to pasture again. A busy day, but everyone was back in camp early to make preparation for the Sabbath on the morrow.

It was getting late, and the evening meal was hurriedly prepared and eaten. From that point on, at sunset, everything done and said was in observance of the Sabbath.

The first day of the week dawned bright and clear, not too cold, and Reuben arrived with his contingent before the breakfast dishes had been put away. Soon everyone left, except Mary and Joseph, to go to their designated stations to register. It took some quite a while, others not so long, so they returned to the stable at all hours. About the ninth hour the last couple straggled in.

At the supper hour that night it was agreed that Barabbas's father would lead the caravan back to Nazareth. It would leave Bethlehem, pick up the people who had stayed in Jerusalem, and be back home by the next Sabbath. Joseph's parents were to take his cart and ox with them.

On being asked what he would do, Barabbas replied, "I've got to get back to the shop in Jerusalem and start earning my keep. I'll stay around here tomorrow while Mary and Joseph take Jesus and go register. I'll leave Judas here to help look after Joab's stock and help Mary and Joseph move out of the stable and into a house some place in town. Then he's got to get back to tentmaking. When Mary and Joseph start home they can make it all right with Hiram. Reuben and I will see that they get in on a good caravan." Thus did the plans work out.

CHAPTER
TWENTY-ONE

Barabbas had been aware when he got up that morning that this was the eighth day, so when they heard someone enter the shop about noon, they were not surprised to see Mary, Joseph, and the baby. The baby was very fretful, and Barabbas could tell Mary had been crying. He looked at Joseph and raised his eyebrows.

"She's been suffering with the boy," Joseph said in answer to Barabbas's unspoken question. He grinned, "She should have had a girl!"

Mary frowned at him, hugged Jesus close, and snuffled.

"We're going over to Ain Karim and spend a few days with Zechariah, Elizabeth, and baby John. Mary wants to see him, and to show off her baby. And maybe Elizabeth can give her some comfort about this," pointing with his chin at Jesus.

"Have you moved out of the stable yet?" asked Reuben.

"Have the promise of a place next week," answered Joseph. "It has a building attached where I can open a carpenter shop. Joab says there are good prospects for the kind of work I do. We'll send Judas back in a few days."

Barabbas was startled. "Open a carpenter shop? In Bethlehem? What about Nazareth?"

"Mary says she wants to stay close to Jerusalem so Jesus will be near the temple. We'll be back here for his dedication in a few days."

During all this time Mary had not uttered a word. She was over at the door now, in the sunshine, gently bouncing Jesus in her arms and crooning sleepy songs.

"Guess we better be on our way. When we come back through, we'll have the dedication ceremony. I'll come over and let you two know." With that, Joseph joined Mary at the door and they left.

Barabbas grinned ruefully and took up his needle. *A baby can sure change your life*, he thought.

A few days later Joseph stopped by the shop to bring Barabbas and Reuben up to date on what was going on. He was on his way to Bethlehem to check on the availability of the house and carpenter shop. He had already been to the temple and arranged for the baby's dedication service on the day after tomorrow. It would be on the sixth day, at the sixth hour, would last about an hour, and that would give them time to get back to Bethlehem before the beginning of the Sabbath. Yes, the baby was no longer sore and fretful, and Mary was in a better frame of mind. With a hurried, "We'll see you at the dedication," Joseph left.

Zechariah, Elizabeth, baby John, Reuben, Barabbas, Levi, and a few curious onlookers were present at the dedication. Judas had come over from Bethlehem, accompanied by the older shepherd who had visited the stable on the night of Jesus' birth. Zechariah had a part in the ceremony, and Mary and Joseph were justly proud of Jesus' behavior during the entire proceedings.

After the ceremony the people from Ain Karim and Bethlehem left quickly, and affairs in the tentmaking shop slowly began to settle down to a more or less normal routine.

Judas came back to work several days later. Mary, Joseph, and Jesus had moved out of the stable and into the house and carpenter shop, about a quarter mile closer to Bethlehem. Being that near the Red Lion Inn, Hiram was kept with Joab's stock, and he seemed content. Joab's wife had assigned Jesse and Daniel the job of keeping the stable clean. This drew some protests from those two, but with younger brothers coming after them, they had the prospect of aging out and passing that job on to others. The crowd of revelers had straggled out of the Red Lion, Joab had been somewhat compensated for repairs he had had to make, and his business was back to normal. Joseph had put up a sign to advertise the carpenter shop and was picking up a few customers. Barabbas was gratified at hearing Judas's report and thought, *Now I can get back to work.* And he didn't have tentmaking in mind.

Barabbas sought and had a conference with Levi within a few days. The first concern of Barabbas was Reuben. It was agreed that he should stay in the shop. It was to be very obvious that he was a partner, half owner, manager, and primary decision-maker. This precluded him from any cell association, activity, or even knowledge. It was Barabbas's desire that Reuben be absolutely squeaky clean, that no taint of brigand activity could touch him. Some of them in the past had been caught red-handed and, as a rule, they usually brought someone else down by association. Barabbas didn't want that to happen. Levi, of course, could see the advantage of this concept.

For himself, Barabbas wanted to be known as Reuben's partner, half owner of the business, but primarily the outside man. Someone had to beat the bushes for business, deliver the finished products, and if possible, follow up to see that the products were satisfactory. This gave him the opportunity to mix the businesses of tentmaking and brigands.

They had just about ceased their operations when Caesar's decree about the registrations was posted. Levi thought they could now resume, but with a little more care regarding recruitment.

Barabbas did deliver the goods made up by Reuben, Seth, and Judas in their shop. He did follow up on customers who were using their goods, to see that they were happy campers. He did make calls, seeking new business.

And some of these calls were at the various gates of the city, where travelers, transients, and other buyers and sellers were wont to pass by or loiter about. This was where his brigand work came into play. But unlike his previous activity of this sort, he now was more perceptive, a bit more cautious, about the ones he targeted for potential troublemakers, rebels, or possible brigands. As he and Levi had discussed, some—even many—of these city-gate layabouts were opportunists looking for a personal, temporary profit. They had no cause but their own. They didn't care whether the Romans, Greeks, or Tartars were in charge, just "What's in it for me?"

True, any trouble for Herod was a thing to be desired, but Barabbas tried to steer clear of any obvious entanglements with people of this sort. With that in mind, Barabbas, in conversation with someone else but in the hearing of others, would drop tidbits of information that would prompt an aspiring troublemaker to get busy making trouble.

So the tentmaking business prospered, trouble spots erupted from time to time throughout Jerusalem and its environs, and the numbers of the cells slowly increased.

Meanwhile, there was much visitation going on between Jerusalem, Bethlehem, and Ain Karim. The tentmakers had business in Bethlehem, so Barabbas was a fairly frequent visitor of Mary, Joseph, and the carpenter shop. It was not unusual for Mary, Jesus, and Hiram to stop by the tentmakers' shop on their way to visit Zechariah, Elizabeth, and John. When this happened, Mary usually had the noon meal with Barabbas and Reuben, then went on to Ain Karim. She would spend one or two nights with Elizabeth, then stop again with Reuben and Barabbas on the way back to Bethlehem.

CHAPTER
TWENTY-TWO

It was another winter. Barabbas had been out on a delivery and had come back into the shop, headed toward the kitchen to prepare a meal. Mary, Joseph, and Jesus were coming in today on their way to Ain Karim. As he passed the cutting table, he saw Judas cutting a pattern. This was nothing new, but it was something different. Every time Barabbas had seen Judas cut a pattern, he had cut as far as he could reach, then walked around the table and finished the cut from the other side. This time he had stretched legs, body, and arms and completed the cut without circling the table. Barabbas stopped abruptly. Judas looked up to see what he wanted, heard nothing, and went back to his work.

"Judas, how long have you been doing that?" he asked.

"Doing what? Cutting patterns? 'Bout two, two and a half years. Why?"

"I know how long you've been working here. I mean, how long have you been stretching across the table instead of walking around it?"

Judas straightened up and grinned at him.

"I don't know. I could all of a sudden do it. What's the matter? Don't you expect a boy to grow?"

"I don't expect a boy to grow into a man overnight," retorted Barabbas. "The last time I saw you cut a pattern, you had to walk around the table."

"That was sometime last year. You haven't been in here that much. Here come Mary, Joseph, and Jesus. Did you know Jesus was walking—I mean running? I never saw him walk."

Everyone looked up as they came through the door. When a two-year-old boy was in a room full of needles, all kinds of cutting tools, and other hazards, someone had to keep him within reach.

Mary scooped him up. "Jesus and I are going to the temple," she said. "When are you going to feed us?"

"Little over an hour," Barabbas replied. "I had started to the kitchen when I saw that Judas had grown up. Had to talk to him about that. Look at the light on his face coming through the window. He's going to have to start shaving!"

Judas blushed and ducked his head.

Mary looked at Barabbas, put her finger across her lips, and shook her head. He looked at Judas and realized he had embarrassed him and instantly regretted it.

"Why don't you take Judas with you to the temple? He can help you keep up with that youngster, and Joseph can help me in the kitchen."

"Sounds like a good idea. Judas, can you leave work for an hour?"

Judas looked over at Reuben, the question in his eyes.

Reuben had been plying his needle but also listening to all the chitchat and knew Judas would like to go with Mary and Jesus.

"Yeah, go on with her. She can use some help. First, bring Hiram 'round back and give him some feed. Better put him in a stall, or he'll wind up in the temple!"

Judas gave Reuben a grateful look and hustled out to do his bidding.

As Joseph and Barabbas were preparing the meal, Joseph stopped a moment and said, "We had some company day before yesterday."

"Yeah?" answered Barabbas. "Who was it?"

"I'm going to wait until Mary gets back and let her tell you. It's a little like the night Jesus was born. Will Reuben, Seth, and Judas be eating with us?"

Barabbas thought for a moment. "You know, I've talked to Reuben about all this stuff—well, not everything, but he knows about the shepherds. So does Judas; he was there. But if this is strange, odd, I'd like for Reuben to hear it. He's a wise man," Joseph smiled "and I want him to know what's going on. Go in the shop and tell him to eat with us. We've got some business to discuss. And why did you grin at me just now?"

"I'll go tell him," and over his shoulder as he walked away, "It was a term you used."

Mary, Jesus, and Judas returned later than expected, and Barabbas was keeping the meal warm in the indoor clay oven.

"I've seen Jesus walk," stated Judas as Jesus ran down the aisle toward the kitchen. "First time."

"Where did the youngster walk?" asked Barabbas.

"In the temple," said Judas. "As we got to the door from the courtyard his mother reminded him: 'Remember, this is a Holy place and we don't run in here.' He walked from then on until we got back out in the courtyard. We passed a door to a room, an open door, where some of the scribes and rabbis were reading a scroll aloud. Bless me if he didn't stop to listen. Someone saw him standing there after a bit and got up and shut the door."

"Did he make any comment?" asked Barabbas facetiously.

"No, but he looked like he wanted to."

"Go on and get your dinner, and tell Reuben to come on—we're ready," said Barabbas as he gave Judas a slap on his backside.

As they started eating, Joseph spoke to Mary, "I told Barabbas about us having company."

"You said you had company. You didn't tell me anything."

Joseph purposely ignored Barabbas and spoke to Mary again. "I told him it would be better if you told what happened. You were there when they came in. I was in the shop."

CHAPTER
TWENTY-THREE

"Barabbas, Reuben, it was strange, like when the shepherds came. These three men appeared at the house—you should have seen them. They were dressed in rich robes—very colorful—turbans, and slippers, not sandals. It came out later that they had changed clothes in Jerusalem. They told a strange story about being way, way off in the east and seeing a bright star. Each man was in a different country, each saw the star, followed it, and the three met in Armenia, wherever that is.

"When the star stopped—I guess it was over Bethlehem—they went into Jerusalem. When they found out Herod was king, they went some place, bathed, changed clothes, and went to see him. They told him a baby had been born to be King of the Jews. He asked them when they saw the star, and they told him they had been following it for almost two years. They said King Herod tried to appear very calm and friendly, but they could tell he was nervous, upset.

"King Herod called in some of his advisors and asked them where this Jewish king was to be born. One of them, a rabbi, told him Bethlehem. Herod told them to find the child, do whatever they came to do, and to come back to the palace and tell him where he is. So they came to Bethlehem and found us. Have you ever heard such a story?"

Mary stopped to take a breath, and Barabbas noticed he nor Reuben had eaten a bite during this whole recital. Joseph, on the other hand, had finished his meal.

Mary, Barabbas, and Reuben began to eat, but it was evident none of the three knew or cared what they were doing.

"What then?" asked Reuben.

"They asked if they could see the child," said Mary. "He was in the shop with Joseph, so I had them sit down and went to get them. Jesus was a mess—wood shavings on his clothes, in his hair. Didn't look much like a king, but beautiful. And you know, when he and Joseph came in, they stood up, walked over to him, knelt before him, and bowed down."

Barabbas had stopped eating again. "And what did Jesus do?" he asked.

"He looked like a king!" his mother answered softly.

The room was quiet for some moments, all lost in their own thoughts.

"Then they gave him some gifts," said Joseph, "talked among themselves in a strange tongue, thanked us, bowed again to Jesus, and left."

"But," added Mary, "they said they were not going back to see Herod. Said for us to be careful. That's why we are going to Ain Karim. We want to see what Elizabeth and Zechariah make of this."

"Has Jesus asked questions or talked about this?" asked Reuben.

"No, not a word." Mary paused for a moment. "You know, it's almost as if he expected it or knew it was going to happen."

She continued, "When I said he looked like a king, I didn't mean he looked haughty, arrogant, like Herod looks when he appears out on the palace balcony. He was smiling, confident, so sure of himself. I wish you could have seen him."

Quietness again. None of them had anticipated anything like this, not this long after the boy's birth.

Joseph broke the silence. "Barabbas, we've been so long at this meal, you're going to have to clean up. We've got to be on our way. We hope we haven't kept you two too long from your work. We'll stop by on our way back to Bethlehem."

By this time Jesus was nodding over his plate. Joseph picked him up in his arms, Mary went to the stable to get Hiram, and they were on their way.

Reuben went into the shop, and Barabbas set the kitchen to rights, puzzling over the story Mary had told. He couldn't fit it into the scheme of the things he knew. Reuben was smart; he would ask him. Reuben was "wise" he had said to Joseph—wise man—wise men, those three were. That's why Joseph had smiled when I called Reuben a wise man. *I hope Zechariah can put this together*, he thought.

CHAPTER
TWENTY-FOUR

arabbas was holding forth at the south gate when, ever alert to his surroundings, he saw Judas come through the gate. He finished his conversation and, without being obtrusive, looked at the sun, said something about an appointment, and casually took his leave. Passing through the gate into the city he walked up the main thoroughfare a short distance, took two right turns, and found himself in a small marketplace. There he loitered about until Judas came alongside.

"You've got to get back to the shop quick," he said.

"What's up?" Barabbas asked.

"Don't know. Joseph came in, got Reuben to one side for a minute or two, and Reuben told me to drop everything and go look for you. I went to the west gate first, then the south."

"Well, let's go. We'll get back on the main road. It's more direct."

Barabbas wanted to run but didn't. Sometimes Caesar's legions would stop a running man, question him about why he was running, and oft times would hold him for hours. Barabbas had not lived in Jerusalem for almost three years without picking up some knowledge of what to expect.

When they reached the shop, Barabbas went in the back door and stayed in the kitchen. Judas went in at the front and saw Joseph standing off to one side while Reuben and Seth were talking with a customer. He looked at Joseph, nodded toward the back, and moved over to his worktable. Joseph walked slowly through the shop and disappeared into the kitchen.

After the men embraced, Barabbas sat down in a chair and leaned back on the two back legs. The chair creaked and popped under the weight but held together. Joseph continued to stand, pacing a bit, which indicated to Barabbas that he was worried, upset.

"Old friend, you got a problem?" he asked.

"Yeah, I got a problem," Joseph answered. "You're going to have to help us get out of the city tonight."

"Oh? Well, tell me about it. Who have you, or Hiram, killed? I know Jesus and Mary haven't done anything." He grinned.

Joseph looked at Barabbas and smiled briefly.

"Guess I had better start at the beginning," he said. "We got to Zechariah's house about midafternoon, and he was in the temple, performing his duties. He didn't get home that night, Elizabeth said that wasn't unusual, so we said nothing about the wise men. . . ." A quick look and a smile at Barabbas. "Did you figure that out?"

Chapter Twenty-Four

Barabbas nodded.

"He came in about noon, the mamas had fed the boys and put them down for a nap, so while we were eating we told them about the men following the star, going by the palace to see Herod—all that stuff. Zechariah was sort of disturbed but didn't know what it all meant. We talked until late and went to bed. That night, last night, Gabriel came again." Pacing, he gave Barabbas a quick look.

"Same man, same appearance?"

Joseph nodded. "Same clothes. Clean, but the same. I described him to Zechariah. *He* said it was the same man who appeared to him in the temple and told him about baby John. Anyway, Gabriel said Herod was on a rampage. The wise men had not come back to tell him where 'The King of the Jews' was and he's going to start a search for him. To make sure he gets the right one, he's seeking all two- to three-year-old boys in Bethlehem and is having them put to death. We are to take Jesus and go to Egypt, leaving tonight, and stay until Herod dies. Gabriel will let us know when to return. Zechariah is afraid our neighbors in Bethlehem will tell these searchers of our visits back and forth between Bethlehem and Ain Karim and that Herod's dragnet might include baby John. He's making arrangements with a caravan today to send Elizabeth and John to Nazareth until the heat's off. Jesus, Mary, and I are going to leave Ain Karim as soon as I get back, presumably for Bethlehem.

"Find us a place to hide out until late tonight, then lead us out of the city, and we'll be on our way. Have I overlooked anything?"

"Looks like you've got it covered," Barabbas answered. "Come in by the west gate as usual. Judas will be there and will guide you to the place I have in mind. Off with you! Get cracking!"

As Joseph started out the back door, Barabbas cautioned, "Walk, don't run!"

Barabbas went to the door and looked out into the shop. Reuben, Seth, and Judas were busy at their worktables. No customers in at the moment. He stepped through the door, out into the shop area, and paused. The ever-vigilant Judas looked up. Barabbas pointed at Reuben and went back into the kitchen.

When Reuben came in, Barabbas was at the food cabinet, laying out food supplies, water skins, and cooking utensils.

"What's up?" Reuben asked, alarm in his voice. "You been spotted?"

"No, nothing like that," he replied. "It's Jesus, Mary, and Joseph."

As he continued to gather supplies, he related to Reuben the story he had heard from Joseph. Reuben listened intently as he began to help Barabbas assemble and sort out the gear.

"You'll have to go with them." A statement, not a question.

"Yes. Joseph is capable enough, but he hasn't had the experience out on the trail that I've had. And he doesn't dare go home to try to get this stuff together. We'll need a small tent and some tent cloth to make up three packs. Will you go get that for me? One for me, one for Joseph, and one for Hiram. Wish we had that backrest gizmo that Mary rode on coming down from home for the registration, but it's in Bethlehem."

Reuben went out into the shop to get the tent and pack cloth, and Barabbas began a meticulous inspection of the assembled goods to see if he had missed anything he had to

have, and also to see if there was anything he could do without. He discovered there were items in both categories.

He continued with the selection process, and Reuben
returned with the tent and pack cloth, his needle and thread.
As Barabbas formed and shaped up the three packs, Reuben
cut and sewed on the backpacking straps. As they worked
they talked: "Get word to Levi, and somehow get word to
the people in Nazareth. Get Joseph's tools and other things
from his shop in Bethlehem, but under no circumstance, tell
anyone where we are going."

"Let it be known we went out the east gate," said Barabbas.
"We will go out that way and later circle to the southeast.
And I forgot, Elizabeth will get word to the kin in Nazareth.
She will tell them she has no idea where we went."

So the plans were made; packs assembled; and Barabbas,
Reuben, and Judas carried them to a hideout the brigands
used from time to time. Barabbas knew a watchman was
there—always was—but he never showed himself. Judas hurried off to the west gate to wait for Jesus, Mary, and Joseph.

As they waited, Barabbas and Reuben continued to talk
in low, guarded whispers about the tentmaking, what to say
if inquiries were made as to Barabbas's whereabouts, what to
do and say to the people in Bethlehem, on and on, until
some time after midnight Barabbas heard the *clop, clop, clop*
of Hiram's hoofbeats. As they came in, he was gratified to see
that neither Mary, Joseph, nor Hiram were burdened with
much of a pack. There was a minimum of conversation and
no time wasted. Reuben went the rounds, giving Barabbas,
Joseph, and Mary a bear hug, and a light kiss on Jesus' cheek.
Then he faded away into the shadows.

Judas whispered, "I'll go out the gate with you."

"Good idea," whispered Barabbas. "Four adults and a donkey could be confusing. We'll keep the baby under wraps."

The trek across the city, from west to east gate, was long, taking little more than an hour. Out the east gate Barabbas turned north and started around the city.

"Why north?" whispered Judas.

"Lost my mind. Wasn't thinking," muttered Barabbas. "We go east a bit, we're going toward Bethlehem. Won't do. More tracks this way to get lost in. When we reach the north side, you go back in. We'll go on around and on our way."

As they neared the main north-south road, Barabbas was not surprised to hear traffic on the road, for traders, merchants, and drovers moved in and out of the city constantly. Barabbas halted the little group.

"We will wait here until there's a break in traffic, then cross without being seen." To Judas: "You go on, fade into a group, and get on back home. You've been a valuable help, Judas. You're not a boy any more; you are man!" He almost crushed Judas's ribs. Then hugs and thanks from Joseph and Mary. When she kissed him goodbye he could feel the tears on her face. As he turned away, he could feel his own tears mingle with hers.

There soon came a break. They reached the road and turned toward Jerusalem for a short distance. Then Mary, riding Hiram and carrying Jesus, turned off to the southwest. About two hundred yards beyond, Joseph turned off to join them. Two hundred yards further Barabbas turned.

When they reached the west-to-east road into the city using the same ruse to cover their tracks, they were well south of Jerusalem and on their way to Egypt in accordance with the instructions of the man called Gabriel.

CHAPTER
TWENTY-FIVE

H aving had so much to do and thus getting such a late start, Barabbas did not feel they were far enough away from Jerusalem to be safe, but neither did he want them to be seen on the road. As it began to lighten in the east he looked for a likely place to leave the road and find a more or less secluded spot to spend the day. He soon found some semblance of a trail not recently traveled, winding off to the east between some low hills. Here he and Joseph put up the tent, rigged a sun shelter for Joseph and himself, gave Hiram a rub down, and took first watch while the others slept. They did a minimum of cooking that day. As they discussed their plight, Barabbas suggested that after the night's travel plus one more, they should be safe enough to travel by day from then on.

As twilight came on, the men took down the tent and made up the packs. Mary prepared a light meal, and Barabbas walked out to scout the road while he could still see for some distance. Seeing nothing that should give them concern, he made his way back to the campsite, put their gear together, and they made their way back to the main road.

Reuben, ever thoughtful and innovative, had fashioned a tent-cloth backpack for the boy Jesus. Straps and ties to fit the back and shoulders of the carrier, a seat and leg holes to fit the boy, all put together with convenience in mind, was a real boon for foot travelers with a child. Mary walked with Hiram. Joseph, on the other side, carried Jesus, and Barabbas ranged from front to back, not really expecting any, but on lookout for trouble.

They traveled through the night, stopping to rest at about three-hour intervals. After each rest stop, Joseph and Barabbas swapped off, Joseph doing the ranging from front to back and Barabbas carrying Jesus in the backpack.

It was on this trip down into Egypt that, to Jesus, Barabbas became "Babbas." The boy had been a fast learner and began to walk and talk early on. When other children in Bethlehem began saying words, Jesus began putting sentences together. When the other children began putting sentences together, Jesus was asking questions and reasoning out answers. He had never lisped, stuttered, had much trouble with saying words, or given to baby talk.

But he couldn't, or wouldn't, say Barabbas. His mother and father had worked with him, sounding out a syllable at a time, urging him to get it right. It always came out "Babbas."

Barabbas couldn't care less. He grinned, and enjoyed answering to Babbas.

As dawn began to appear, Barabbas started looking for a likely spot to spend the day. He soon found it and followed the same procedure as the day before: Set up the tent and have a skimpy breakfast. Soon Jesus, Mary, and Joseph were fast asleep in the tent. Barabbas moved away and found a spot from which he could watch the camp and the logical approach from the road. He sat down with his back against a tree and began to assess their situation.

Last night they had met one small group going toward Jerusalem, and another group of six men had passed them going west. Each time, meeting the group or being over-taken by the other, the two groups had stopped for a brief conversation.

No one in either group had shown any particular interest in the other. Barabbas estimated they had traveled ten miles the first night, due to the late start, and maybe twenty to twenty-five miles last night. Thirty-five miles from Jerusa-lem. Not far if old Herod knew where they were headed.

Let's see, today is Thursday, he thought. *We travel twenty to twenty-five miles tonight, that puts us maybe sixty miles from Jerusalem. Getting better, but we lay up during the day; the Sab-bath starts at sundown. Can't travel that night—or the next day. If Herod has some of Caesar's legions out on a search, they don't observe the Sabbath. Hmm, the ox may be in the ditch.*

We're thirty-five miles out. Tonight we'll make it maybe sixty. Travel Friday night and we're close to a hundred miles away. Think we'd be safe enough then. We could lay over a day and night, then travel daytime. Won't be so conspicuous.

Don't know where or how far Egypt is. Or what we'll do when we get there. Mary will say, "God won't let anything hap-pen to Jesus." Barabbas smiled wryly. *I don't want anything to happen to the rest of us!* Thus Barabbas ruminated until about midday, when Joseph came out to take over the watch.

Barabbas slept until late afternoon, then while Mary and Joseph prepared supper he told them of his reasoning about still being within reach of a military search party, the necessity he felt for traveling on the Sabbath, their ignorance of just where they were going, and so on.

"In other words," said Mary, grinning at him, "The ox is in the ditch."

Barabbas grinned sheepishly.

She always could read my mind, he thought to himself.

Joseph had to chuckle, and Jesus looked from one to the other, trying to figure out what was going on.

"We have taught Jesus the Ten Commandments and have emphasized how we should observe the Sabbath," Mary said. "You," looking at Joseph, "and Barabbas finish getting supper." To Jesus: "Come sit on my lap and listen to me." The boy settled on her lap, back straight as an arrow, and watched her eyes and lips intently.

"You know God said, 'Remember the Sabbath and keep it holy—don't do any work'?" Jesus nodded. "Well," she continued, "what is work? Some people who teach, who make rules and laws, have carried the word *work* so far as to be a burden, even to be ridiculous. Suppose on the Sabbath a strong wind comes up, blows open the door to the sheepfold. A little lamb gets out and wanders off. We look out the window and see what has happened. Do we keep the Sabbath, don't do any work?" The boy's eyes are big, troubled.

"No," Mary answered her own question. "We go close and fasten the gate tight so it won't blow open. Then we count the sheep, and lo, one is missing." The boy's eyes get bigger, and he's obviously more troubled. "We've already done a little work, broken the Sabbath, according to some people. Do we go back to the house, sit down, and forget the little lamb?"

Jesus gave a violent shake of his head, and Mary hugged him tight. "No," she said. "We go out, try to follow its tracks, call it by name, and seek until we find it. Then we pick up the little lost lamb," Jesus smiled, "bring it back to the sheepfold and put it with its mama.

"Or as Barabbas says," she sounded out Ba-rab-bas, syllable by syllable—the boy shot him a quick look and turned back to the storyteller. "We have a loveable old ox. He pulls our plow, hauls our water, does lots of things. One Sabbath day he gets out of his pen, goes grazing out on a steep hillside, stumbles and falls into a ditch." She continued, "We hear him bellowing and thrashing around, see his legs waving in the air, trying to turn over so he can get up. Do we keep the Sabbath and stay in the house, don't work?" More head shaking and more hugging. "No, we get some help, go get the poor fellow out, lead him back to the pen, and maybe give him some water.

"Now," she went on, "when we were at Aunt Elizabeth's, an angel came to Daddy in the night and told him some bad people were out to do us some harm. He said for us to leave Ain Karim that night—don't go back to Bethlehem even. That is the reason Ba-rab-bas helped us leave in the dark. He thinks we are not far enough away to be safe, so we need to travel, to work on the Sabbath. Do you understand?"

Jesus nodded his head and looked at Barabbas. "We got to get the ox outta th' ditch!"

Mary, Joseph and Barabbas laughed until they had tears in their eyes.

CHAPTER
TWENTY-SIX

They ate supper, packed the gear, and were soon on the road again. As on the previous night, Joseph took first watch with the boy in the backpack. Mary walked with Hiram, and Barabbas was ahead, out of sight in the early darkness. He was so far ahead that when he heard voices and other sounds of travel approaching from the rear he stopped stock-still, and not hearing Hiram's hoofbeats he instinctively stepped off the road into the shadows, ducked, ran about fifteen feet and squatted behind a bush. He peered through the brambles and noted that there were six men, traveling light and fast.

He heard a voice: "There were two men last night. Wonder where the other one is?"

"Bet he's not far," said another voice. Another voice answered these two, but they were too far away or it was too low for Barabbas to catch. He waited until he heard Hiram's *clip clop* before he stood and joined his companions.

Joseph said, "You slipped off the road." A statement, not a question.

"Yeah, and the same group passed us last night."

"I know. Jesus recognized one of 'em."

Barabbas was startled. "He did?! How'd he do that?"

Jesus answered for himself, "He was black-headed, like you, but had a wide, white streak in his hair. In the back," he added.

Barabbas looked at the boy in wonder. He had noticed a white streak—a saber cut maybe?—but he didn't think anyone else had.

"Are these the bad people, Babbas?" he asked.

"I don't think so. At least, not the ones the angel was talking about."

Jesus sensed the concern in the looks and voices of the two men, "But are there other bad people?"

"Yes, Jesus. There are bad people all over," answered Joseph. "But don't you worry." He looked around and smiled at the boy. "We've got angels looking after us!"

He looked at Barabbas. "Think we had better stop early and give this some thought?"

Barabbas nodded in approval. "For a carpenter, you make a first-rate trail hand." He continued, "I don't think they'll do anything tonight since they're not sure where I am. We'll stop about midnight, wait, and see what happens tomorrow."

Barabbas did not go far ahead again and was very much on the alert for unexpected noises. When the position of the stars began to indicate midnight, he led the others off the road a short distance and instructed them to wait while he explored a bit. It was almost an hour before he returned, but he led them back on the road and into a secluded and suitable spot for a layover. Barabbas and Joseph agreed that it would be best to sleep out rather than put up the tent. As usual, Barabbas took first watch, but due to the tension and uncertainty of what morning might bring, no one slept very well.

Friday morning dawned bright and clear. While Mary and Joseph prepared breakfast, Barabbas left on another exploration. Again he was gone about an hour. The others had eaten. As he ate his late breakfast he made his report: "There were a few people on the road, going both directions, but nothing unusual about any of them. No, there was no sign of anyone who might be of the party of six. Yes, let's just wait here. Let somebody else make the first move. I didn't get out on the road, but our tracks leaving the road coming in here are plain to see if anyone is looking for them. I'm going out a little way, where I can hear better. I'll take Hiram with me, he hears better than I do. Mary, why don't you tell Jesus some stories."

Barabbas had his staff, a sling with a pouch of smooth stones, and two wicked-looking knives. Taking Hiram by the halter he led him out, away from the sound of the camp but not out of sight, and sat down on a huge boulder embedded in the ground. There was a lot of bushy undergrowth all around, about waist high, and they were all out of sight and sound from the road.

As he waited and Hiram slept, Barabbas began his ruminations again. *That crowd has an interest in us for some reason. Don't think it's robbery, for we are obviously not wealthy. Or would they think we are and are trying to look poor? They passed us, pulled off the road like we've been doing so we would get ahead, then passed again for a second look. An old brigand trick! Now I wonder—even if Joseph and I get the chance, we can't kill a spy if he comes. The other five would come looking, and we couldn't handle them. This is something we're going to have to talk our way out of.*

Barabbas, sitting in the warm sunshine appeared to be asleep. His head had drooped, eyes partly closed, but he was looking carefully, intently from side to side when Hiram suddenly raised his head, his ears shot forward and he snuffled a long breath. Barabbas didn't move anything but his eyes and looked quickly in the direction Hiram was staring. No movement at all. Hiram raised his head higher and pawed the ground impatiently. Still no movement. Finally, a quiet, "Ho! The camp."

Barabbas raised his head and turned toward the voice: "You've got the camp!"

"Mind if I stand up? I don't want a rock in my skull or a knife in my gizzard."

"Come on in," Barabbas answered, "but make it slow and easy."

A figure arose from behind the bushes, very slowly, some forty feet away. He was small of stature, shaggy haired, bearded, and scantily clad.

"I don't have a staff, too clumsy for a sneak," he smiled briefly, "but I have a knife. Shall I pitch it to you?"

Barabbas answered, "No, come on in. You could have two knives—or more!"

The man smiled again and approached slowly, his hands and arms held out well away from his sides. Barabbas stood up, edged carefully around the rock where he had been sitting and with his staff ready, he awaited his approach. With a hand sign, he stopped the sneak about ten feet out.

"Joseph!" Barabbas called loudly.

"Yeah," came back the answer.

"Come over here. We need some conversation."

Joseph soon appeared, carrying his staff and seeing Barabbas and the sneak facing each other across the rock, he took a wide turn and joined Barabbas.

"What's going on?" he asked.

"Don't know," Barabbas answered, "but we don't want to leave Mary and the boy alone. Let's go back to camp, and we won't have to hear the story but once." To the stranger: "I'd like to disarm you. You know the drill?"

The stranger smiled again, nodded and turned his back, holding his arms and hands out shoulder high. Barabbas and Joseph walked around the rock, and while Barabbas patted him down, finding only one knife, Joseph stood by, alert for any overt move on the stranger's part.

"Now," said Barabbas, slipping the stranger's knife in his belt, "let's walk back to camp. And please," to the stranger, "be careful around the boy."

They approached the camp, and Mary and Jesus looked up expectantly, no sign of alarm on either face.

As they sat down, Mary arose and said, "You men must be thirsty. I'll get you something to drink. Would you like something to eat?"

"No, not yet," answered Barabbas, "and call Hiram in, will you?"

Barabbas was still uncertain about the other five men and had positioned himself so he could react quickly if need be. And he wanted Hiram on watch with him.

As Hiram came in and found some water and food available, Mary sat back down beside Jesus and pulled him on her lap. Barabbas looked at the stranger and nodded.

Chapter Twenty-Six

"My name is Amos," he began, "and we have been looking for you."

"What do you mean, looking for us?" asked Joseph. "And what for?"

"We were looking for two men, a woman and a child," answered Amos. "The first night we passed, we saw two men, a woman, but no child. We had passed two other groups that partly filled the bill, even to the donkey. So we arranged to pass again. We saw one man, a woman, and a child. We still were not sure, so I was sent to scout your party to make sure you were or were not the people we are looking for. I was just trying to get as close as I could, a matter of sneaking pride I suppose. But the donkey, Hiram, spotted me. He's a smart jackass."

Hiram's ears shot forward, then laid back. He quit eating and snorted loudly.

Amos looked quickly at Hiram, then at the chuckling party of four.

"He's a very smart donkey and objects, sometimes rather violently, to the term *jackass*," Mary explained. "But why are you looking for us, or are you sure we are *it*?"

"I'm sure you're it. The six of us work for Levi," Barabbas let out a long breath, "and have for a long time. He has a lot of business interests, and we help look after his properties, keep them repaired, keep down vandalism, chastise and punish culprits, use some strong-arm measures at times." He looked at Jesus and back to Barabbas. "I don't want to be any more explicit than that."

Barabbas nodded and replied, "I understand and thank you. But what are you to do? What is your mission?"

"Apparently you and your party are important to him, mean a great deal to him. After your tentmaker partner, Reuben, came to him and told him what was going on, he called in Whitey and told him to get six men together, find you, and get you safely to Egypt, to Pelusium."

"Who's Whitey?" asked Jesus.

Amos looked startled. "His name is Saul, named for our first king."

"He spotted the white streak," said Barabbas, by way of explanation.

"Oh," said Amos, and looked at Jesus with greater interest.

"So," asked Barabbas, "shall we join your group and wait out the day and night, or shall we move on as far as we can before nightfall?"

"I think Whitey would like to move on today. Let's join them and see."

As they were breaking camp and packing up, Amos asked, "What do you plan to do about the Sabbath?"

"The ox is in the ditch," stated Jesus.

Mary explained the statement to Amos as they were on their way to join the others. He looked again at Jesus very thoughtfully and with great curiosity.

CHAPTER
TWENTY-SEVEN

Barabbas still had his guard up, and he sensed that Joseph did too. He had been somewhat amazed and gratified at the versatility and acuteness Joseph had shown since this last visit and message from Gabriel—man or angel. He could have fallen apart, could have become a part of the problem. But no, he had met the crisis head on, and Barabbas, walking with Amos in the lead, turned and looked back at Joseph bringing up the rear, alert and ready. He felt a burst of love and appreciation for the man such as he had never felt before. Mary and Jesus were in good hands, and he, Barabbas, had a giant of an ally.

Barabbas came back to the moment at hand. Herod was devious and could use devious people. By quizzing friends and neighbors of Mary and Joseph in Bethlehem he could have learned of the visits to Ain Karim. He also had some very learned people at his beck and call. They could have put two and two together, added up to four, and found the tentmaking shop, Reuben, and the connection to Levi. The man, Barabbas, had a connection with the people who had two, two- to three-year-old boys in Bethlehem and Ain Karim.

Barabbas was nowhere to be seen. The carpenter and his wife and child had disappeared. It all added up to a hurried flight. Find the children and receive a big reward. Some shrewd people could have put together the story Amos had told. Barabbas casually felt around his belted waist for his knives and the one belonging to Amos. They were in place. He took a firmer hold of his staff. If Amos noticed, he gave no indication.

About a mile from where this group had gotten back on the road, Amos slowed his pace, pursed his lips and whistled a perfect birdcall. It was answered almost immediately by a like call from somewhere to their right. He continued about twenty yards, stopped by a break in the bushes that lined the roadside, and looked at Barabbas. "Do you go first or do I?" he asked.

Barabbas looked back past Mary, Jesus, and Hiram, at Joseph, and jerked his head in a "come here" motion. Looking back at Amos and drawing his knife, he replied tersely, "You do."

Amos looked at the knife, looked Barabbas in the eye, smiled briefly, turned, and walked through the gap, Barabbas on his heels and Joseph on his. Mary, purely by instinct, held Hiram back momentarily. Coming out into the open, Barabbas swept the area with a quick glance and saw no one. Joseph ranged up beside him, and they stayed close to Amos as he rounded a little cluster of trees. There in the confines of a lived-in campsite were five men, all looking in their direction but scattered about, two sitting, the others standing, but all seemingly in an attitude of indolent relaxation. Barabbas audibly let out a deep breath.

"I see you found them," said the one Amos had called Whitey.

"They found me," answered Amos. "Or rather, he did," he continued, pointing at Hiram as he, Mary, and Jesus came into view.

The two sitting men scrambled to their feet and all nodded courteously in Mary's direction. One of them spread a mat in an obvious invitation to have a seat.

With introductions made, food and drink offered and accepted, everyone was soon relaxed and at ease, Whitey looked at Amos. "You told them why we are here?"

"Yeah," he answered, and smiling, continued, "When we get back I think you can tell Levi we were not too needful. These two," indicating Joseph and Barabbas, "are two very alert and capable gents. They can take care of themselves."

"That's the opinion I got from Levi," Whitey answered. "But he was afraid they might get swamped by sheer numbers. We'll go on together to Pelusium."

He looked at Barabbas. "Did Amos ask you about traveling tomorrow?"

"The ox is in the ditch," said Amos, smiling at Mary and Jesus.

Whitey looked at Amos.

"She'll tell you," responded Amos, pointing his chin at Mary.

Mary hugged Jesus tight to her side for a moment and told again how they had explained to him the necessity for traveling on the Sabbath.

The men chuckled appreciatively as she concluded, and Amos spoke again, "By the way," looking at Whitey, "he recognized you when we passed the second time."

Whitey gave Jesus a quick glance. "I saw the white streak," Jesus said with a smile.

Whitey rubbed the palm of his hand several times down the back of his head. "I have been told I ought to dye it or cover it up," he said. "But I sort of like it. People see me once, they remember. Sometimes, that's good." He rose to his feet.

"Let's hit the road."

CHAPTER
TWENTY-EIGHT

Neither Barabbas nor Joseph had realized what a strain they had been under. Now, with an additional six men such as they would have picked, given the opportunity, they felt as safe and secure as they would have been in the temple in Jerusalem. Safer! Caesar's legions had been known to go into a Sabbath worship service and pluck some hapless thief from the midst of a congregation. Now they moved more swiftly, started earlier, and traveled later. Campsites seemed to spring up out of the ground, and next morning would disappear into packs just as quickly. Often, during the day and night, Barabbas, Joseph, and Mary would look up, offer a fervent prayer, and bless the name of Levi.

Two days later they were nearing Pelusium when Whitey, spotting a likely camping spot, called a midafternoon halt.

"Time for a conference," he stated, by way of explanation. "Better we should arrive midmorning than at nightfall."

With the camp established; two men preparing the evening meal; the others mending sandals, tents, packs, and other gear; Jesus busy at play; Joseph, Barabbas, Mary and Whitey sat down for a lengthy conference that continued into and through the evening meal.

It began with Whitey's statement and question. "You're in Egypt. Where or in what kind of a place do you want to live—and for how long?"

The discussion went on and on. In Pelusium? Too big? Yeah, too big. What will we do? Carpenter shop? Shepherding? Fishing? Small towns? Isolated areas? How long? Don't know.

Joseph, Mary, and Barabbas learned that all the men had been in Pelusium on other occasions, for Levi had business interests there. Two of the men had lived in Pelusium and were very familiar with the area. Whitey had had business contacts with them while attending to Levi's interests, and had persuaded them to cast their lots with Levi.

As the discussion wore on things began to clarify. Joseph wanted a small village where he could ply his trade. Barabbas wanted the wide-open places, preferably near water and grass, for shepherding. Mary wanted a small village, with female companionship and small children, plus a synagogue and a rabbi.

All the men with Whitey, and including Whitey, were Jewish, but Jews had always been, and still were, a nomadic people. They had been sent by Levi, led by Whitey, to secure the safety and comfort of this little band of four. So the five of them, while busy at their various tasks and while eating their evening meal, had listened with a great deal of interest to all this discussion.

The youngest of the six, Samuel, looking somewhat apologetically at Whitey, spoke up, "I think I know the place. Used to live there. Some of my kin still do."

All eyes were focused on Samuel, making him obviously very self-conscious.

"Where is this place?" asked Whitey. "I thought you were born in Pelusium."

"No," answered Samuel." My father died when I was eleven. My mother married my father's older brother, and we all moved to Pelusium. I had three brothers and two sisters.

A long pause while everyone waited expectantly.

Finally, "Well?" said Whitey, in a gentle tone.

"Oh," said Samuel with a start. "The place!" he gave Whitey a nervous laugh. "It's Succoth, about forty miles southwest of Pelusium. There's a lake nearby, and it's not too far from the Red Sea."

Whitey was not familiar with the place but began trying to picture the geography in his mind.

To Joseph: "I've never been out there, but it may be what you all are looking for." To Samuel: "Could you four," indicating the other three, "take them down there for a look-see? I'll stay in Pelusium with these two and tend to some things for Levi." An afterthought: "You were eleven. Remember how to get there?"

"Oh yeah," Samuel replied. "I've been back since then."

Another thoughtful pause: "We'll get into Pelusium about noon tomorrow, maybe earlier. You four," indicating Barabbas and his group, "can relax, rest up, replenish supplies—whatever." To Samuel: "It'll take two days to

Succoth?" He nodded. "There are shops there? Markets? Synagogue? All the things these people will need?" Samuel nodded again. "About how many people live there?"

Samuel gave it some thought. "Four, maybe five hundred."

Whitey looked his question at Mary and Joseph. Both nodded in assent.

"It's settled then. You four look the place over. If it suits, fine. If not, scout around a bit, see what else may be out there. If nothing fits, come back to Pelusium and we'll ask around and go look again. As for my four," he pointed at his men, "I'll look for them when I see 'em."

He smiled and rose to his feet. "Bedtime," he said, pointing at Jesus asleep with his head in his mother's lap. "We want an early start in the morning."

As Whitey had intimated, they arrived in Pelusium before noon. Joseph, Mary, and Jesus took a room in an inn where Whitey and his men were staying. Barabbas found a stable, checked Hiram in for the rest of the day and night, and made arrangements with the stable owner to stay that night in the haymow.

Then he and Joseph checked their gear, equipment, and supplies, repaired what they could, and went shopping for whatever else was needful.

Next morning, they all met in the inn for an early breakfast. Then the leave-taking got pretty intense. If Barabbas, Joseph, Mary, and Jesus remained in Succoth, or somewhere in that part of the country, they had no idea when or if they would ever see Whitey, Amos, Daniel, and the others again. The care, support, and thoughtfulness of these six men had bound them so deeply in the hearts and minds of this little fugitive band that they could never be forgotten or properly thanked. It was with much shedding of tears, hugs, and an outpouring of expressions of love and good wishes that the four took their leave.

The two days traveling passed without incident. There were very few people on the road, and Samuel proved to be a good guide.

At the end of the second day, as they were approaching Succoth, Samuel began pointing out landmarks and places of interest. When Barabbas pointed out the scarcity of grass, Samuel reassured him: "Oh, that's southeast of the town, toward the water. That's where the sheep are."

As they neared Succoth, Barabbas, Mary, and Joseph were surprised at how like in appearance Succoth was to Nazareth. The terrain, climate, and vegetation was and had been similar to that in Galilee and Judea, but somehow, being in another country, they were expecting something different.

Getting into the village itself, they did find a bit of a language problem. But when they arrived at the home of Samuel's kinfolk, the effusive greetings they received were well understood. After all, wherever the Jews went, they took their language with them.

Samuel's relatives would have welcomed the strangers in any case, but they were especially grateful for those responsible for the visit of one of their own. When they learned that this family of four might possibly settle in and stay for some extended time, they went all out extolling the virtues of their community.

"Yes, we believe a carpenter would be kept fairly busy. . . . Oh, we have an active assembly in our synagogue. . . . We raise a lot of sheep, and the wool merchants from Pelusium make Succoth one of their regular stops. . . . There are many children here. . . . Yes, we are sure you can find a house."

Mary and Joseph were somewhat overwhelmed. Jesus went to sleep. Barabbas was given the names of some sheep owners. All were well fed and taken care of for the night.

The next two days were busy ones for Barabbas and Joseph as they explored possibilities, and Mary and Joseph moved around in the village getting acquainted.

By the third day the refugees from Herod had pooled their information, given their approval of what they had learned, and told Samuel they would like to stay—no more looking around. Samuel was extremely gratified with their decision, and while Mary and Joseph made arrangements for living quarters and a carpenter shop, he took Barabbas out for an extended observation trip of the grazing lands. Barabbas was especially pleased with the proximity of the little lake. It simplified the watering problem and looked promising for fishing.

On the fifth day in Succoth, Samuel and his three companions said their goodbyes and took their leave. It was another sad parting, and Mary, Joseph, Jesus, and Barabbas were again made very much aware of, and thankful for, the love, care, and thoughtfulness of their friends back in Jerusalem.

CHAPTER
TWENTY-NINE

T hings settled down into a normal lifestyle. Joseph had abandoned all his tools back in Bethlehem, but he was able to purchase some in shops and from individuals in Succoth, and also from an occasional caravan or itinerant peddler on the way to or from Pelusium. He had found adequate housing for his family and shop. With no orders for anything, he began to build up an inventory of items he knew someone would soon want or need.

Barabbas loved the outdoors and was particularly fond of sheep. Their helplessness and dependence upon people appealed to him. There was a sheepdog with the flock assigned to him, and with his affinity for animals, he and the dog soon built up a love and respect for each other.

Barabbas missed Reuben and his other friends in Jerusalem, but was reconciled to having to put his brigand work on hold.

Jesus helped. Barabbas dearly loved him, and Jesus loved "Babbas." Barabbas did not bring the sheep in every night, as he and Mary had done at Nazareth. He stayed with them day and night, and only went into the village to replenish his supplies or to take Jesus home.

The first time he went in for supplies, he wheedled Mary into letting him take Jesus back with him. Jesus loved it. He was outdoorsy too. He made friends with the dog and soon learned all the hand signals, but he was too short—low to the ground—for the dog to see. When riding on Barabbas's shoulders, he did very well.

The two had such a good time together and time passed so quickly, that when he heard a sudden sharp "Babbas" he looked quickly at the boy who pointed with his chin. Barabbas looked in that direction and was startled and mortified to see Mary riding up on Hiram, her jaw set and her eyes flashing.

"Do you know how long you've had this boy out here?"

Barabbas hung his head, dug his toe in the ground, looked up, and shook his head. Jesus kept quiet.

"Four days—and nights! And tomorrow is the Sabbath."

"Ox in a ditch," Jesus mumbled.

The tension broke with such gales of laughter that nearby sheep were scattered in fright.

After that, Barabbas kept a short stick handy and cut a notch on it when he and Jesus got up in the morning. When he had three notches, he took the boy home.

For the rest of his life, Barabbas remembered those days on the sheep pastures around Succoth in Egypt as perhaps the happiest of his life. Jesus was growing, in body, mind, and with a vibrant curiosity.

Barabbas took him fishing. He was too small to handle one end of a net, but Barabbas fashioned a stake pole on one end, drove it in the ground, and thus anchored that end of the net. Telling Jesus to hold it steady, he took the other end. Holding the pole upright, he waded out into the water on a wide sweep and onto shore about thirty feet from where he went in. There would be fish trapped in the net as it was pulled ashore, flopping, jumping. Jesus watched big-eyed, straining to hold his end steady. As anxious as he was to get to the fish, he never relinquished his hold on the pole until an "all clear" from Babbas. And he developed a voracious appetite for fish broiled over an open fire.

Jesus and Barabbas would go looking for lost sheep, usually little lambs. With an anxious mama *baaing* incessantly, Barabbas could usually start Jesus toward the "lost" lamb, and he would go in the other direction—but always watching the boy. Soon a happy shout, "Here it is!" and Barabbas would stride over, pretending amazement that Jesus had found the lost one so quickly.

This game had been going on for about six months when one day Barabbas was suddenly brought up short. Out of a clear sky Jesus asked, "Babbas, what was that hand sign you gave Whitey and he made back to you?"

Barabbas had good control of his nerves and didn't turn a hair, but he was so shocked he could hardly breathe. He had thought Whitey might be a brigand, and one day when he thought they were alone, he had flashed him an identification sign. After a little delay, Whitey had flashed him the proper response.

"Any others in the group?" Barabbas had asked.

Whitey had shaken his head, but he was looking some-where past Barabbas, a quizzical look in his eyes. Barabbas had casually turned, as if to walk away from Whitey, and there was Jesus standing in the path. Barabbas had patted him on the head and walked on by.

All this flashed through his mind as Barabbas considered his answer. The truth seemed his only option. "I'm a member of a secret club of men. I wondered if Whitey was a member, so I asked him by a secret hand sign. I couldn't ask him out loud, because if he wasn't a member I didn't want him to know I was. Turned out he is a member, and he told me so with his hand sign. You understand all that?"

Jesus nodded his head slowly. "I think so. I've tried to make the sign, but I'm not sure I'm doing it right. Can you show me?"

Barabbas was stumped for only a moment.

"I don't want to show you that one, nor do I want you to use it—ever. I'll show you one that's better. Should you ever get in trouble, in danger, if you are ever scared and need help, anywhere at any time, and there are people around, do this." Barabbas made the sign. Jesus made the sign. "Again," said Barabbas. He had Jesus make the sign several more times.

"Remember now, don't ever do this just willy-nilly, and never, never show it to anybody. Only when you need help. Never any other time. Got that?"

Jesus nodded.

"Promise?" asked Barabbas, holding up his right hand.

"Double promise," Jesus added for good measure.

"All right!" said Barabbas. "Let's go fishing."

As they were gathering up the fishing gear Barabbas talked to himself again. *That boy is something else. I believe he's making a dolt out of me about the lost sheep. He can see through that farce with his eyes closed. Next time I send him looking for a sheep, it's going to be lost from me, him, and its mama!*

One day Barabbas suggested they take the net out in a boat, and Jesus' eyes lit up in eager anticipation.

Barabbas began to drive the end stake in the ground as usual. "I'll drive it in a little deeper this time since you won't be holding it," although he set it at the same depth as usual.

"Think that'll do?" he asked, his hands on the stake as if trying to shake it.

Jesus put his hands on the stake, halfheartedly pushed and pulled a time or two, and replied," Yep, that'll do." He was looking out toward the boat.

Seeing the expression on the boy's face, Barabbas dropped the heavy end of the maul to the ground, leaned with one hand on the handle, and crossed one foot over the other. He was silent so long, Jesus jerked his attention back to him.

"How long have you known that stake wouldn't budge, even if you were nowhere near it?"

The boy gave him a wide grin. "Ever since the first time, when I saw you struggle and strain, trying to get the thing out of the ground."

Barabbas looked off into the distance a moment. *How dumb can I be?* he thought to himself. *Smarten up, man!*

He looked at Jesus. "Tell you what," he said thoughtfully.

"What?" the boy answered.

"I won't try to fool you anymore. You're too smart for me."

Jesus opened his mouth to interrupt, and Barabbas held up his hand, palm out, and continued. "If I tell you a sheep or a lamb is lost, it's lost and I'm worried. If I tell you a stake might pull loose, it just might. Whatever I tell you, you better believe *I* believe what I'm saying. Something you don't understand, stop me and ask. And we're herding sheep, understand? There are some things I've been doing that you can do. You've got some responsibilities, just like I have. And if I expect too much, tell me, not your mama." They grinned at each other.

"We're going to be completely honest with each other. If I say something dumb, you say, 'Babbas, that's dumb!' Got that?"

"Got that. Now, how do we go fishing in the boat?"

At Barabbas's request, some friends from across the lake had brought them the boat last week, when he had Jesus for three days, and he had taken the boy out on the water, explaining terms, showing him about working oars, using the tiller, and talking about playing out the net as the boat moved.

"Come on, we've got to load the net a certain way, in the stern, so you can play it out. What did I just say?"

"We load the net in the back of the boat, folded so I can push it off as you row out and around, back to shore. And I don't use the tiller, 'cause you can guide with the oars."

"Right you are," answered Barabbas, "Let's stretch out the net."

He worked down through the net to find the pole on the other end, and they walked down the beach, then back to the boat with the pole end, the net stretched out on the sand.

"Now, we put the pole down in the boat, pull the net in, and fold it back and forth, piling it up here." They began piling up the net, stopping to rest at intervals, until Barabbas said, "That's enough, let's push the boat out."

It took some doing to get the boat in the water, and both were wet when they clambered over the side.

"Let me get my breath," said Barabbas as he dropped down on the seat and picked up an oar.

"You fooling me?" asked Jesus, an impish grin on his face.

"No, I'm not fooling you," retorted Barabbas. "We're going to have to get the boat in the water before we load the net. Should've thought of that." He expelled a deep breath and picked up the other oar.

"You ready?" he asked as he settled the oars in the locks and braced his feet.

"I guess," muttered Jesus as he picked up the top fold. "Hope I get this right."

"I'll move slow," said Barabbas. "Watch your feet. Don't let 'em get tangled in the net and pull you over the side."

Jesus gave him a startled look, glanced down at his bare feet, and backed off a bit.

He began to throw off the folds of net but called out over his shoulder, "You fooling me?"

"I've told you. Now you listen and listen good, or you can stay in Succoth seven days a week. I tell you something, I mean it. . . . Look at me," he demanded. Jesus looked and saw fire in his eyes he had never seen before.

"We made a bargain: I tell you something, you believe it. Understand?"

A subdued Jesus nodded his head. "Yes, Babbas. I understand."

Barabbas bent to the oars again. "Throw off some more net," he ordered.

Nothing more was said as Barabbas continued to row slowly in a much wider semicircle than he had been able to walk. Jesus continued to play out the net, wanting to look at Barabbas for a nod or a headshake, but he was too busy. Barabbas rowed just fast enough to keep him humping, and when he beached the boat about fifteen feet from where they went in, the boy was breathing hard.

"Good job, boy, very good. Give me your hand, and I'll swing you ashore. You're too hot to get wet."

Jesus stumbled to the bow and gave his hand to Barabbas who was now standing in the water. He swung him up and out, took two long strides and set his feet on the beach.

Wading back to the boat, Barabbas called back over his shoulder, "Get your breath. I'll get the pole outta' the boat, and we'll pull in some fish!"

He made slow work, pulling the boat farther up on the beach, getting the pole out of the boat, and walking backward, pulling the net.

"Ready? I'll hold the pole. Grip some of the net in your fingers and help me pull."

They walked backward, pulling the net, watching anxiously as more net came ashore.

"Drop what we've got, let's run to the water and pull some more."

Jesus' stubby legs churned as he ran back to the water, waded in, and picked up net with fish flip-flopping around his feet. Barabbas gathered up net and again they walked backward, pulling more net and more fish than they could handle. Jesus was ecstatic.

The boy ought to be a fisherman, thought Barabbas as they finally hauled in all the net, kept all the fish he thought he could clean, and threw the rest back in the lake.

Barabbas began to clean fish while Jesus struggled with the net, stretching it out on the sand to dry, stored the oars, and gathered wood for a cook fire.

That night, two boys, or maybe two men, leaned against a log backrest. Feet to the fire ring, now a bed of coals, stomachs full of broiled fish, stars and moon overhead, night sounds lulling. They cogitated on how good life could be.

Barabbas's conscience had been nagging him ever since his outburst of temper that morning, but he hated to break the companionable silence. However, he knew he should not try to go to sleep until he got it said.

"Boy?"

"Yeah?" lazily.

"I lost my temper this morning. I expect I hurt your feelings. Shouldn't have done that, and I'm sorry. Will you forgive me?"

"Babbas?"

"Yes?"

"That's dumb!"

Barabbas sat up so quickly he startled the dog: "What do you mean, that's dumb?"

"First, tell me about maybe getting my feet tangled up in a net," Jesus responded.

"I've seen a big man playing out a net, throwing out several folds at once because the boat was moving fast. He got careless, feet got tangled, and the net yanked him over the side like a stone out of a sling. 'Course, it was a big, heavy net. But he was a big, heavy man."

Jesus sat up. "Did you, or whoever, get him out of the water?"

"Yeah. But it was close. Like to have drowned."

Jesus lay back against the backrest; "Babbas, I asked you a dumb question, 'Are you fooling me?' I know you love me, look after me, teach me. I love you, and you can't hurt my feelings—for long."

It was dark. Barabbas couldn't see ,but he knew the boy was wearing his grin. "I knew you lost your temper. Mama says that's not nice, but sometimes a good thing. Today's the best day we've ever had, and I love you lots. Can I sleep with you tonight?"

Barabbas swept the boy up in his arms, and as the small, warm, supple body curled up against his, he looked up once more and thanked his lucky stars.

CHAPTER
THIRTY

The three-day visits continued and also the fishing, when shepherding and weather permitted. The fishing proved to be a boon to the people of Succoth.

When Barabbas took Jesus back home after the first boat-fishing experience, they carried the leftover fish they couldn't cook and eat. It was too much for Mary and Joseph so they shared with others. When the others heard Jesus tell of the catch he and Babbas threw back, they decided to be there when the net was pulled in. Many of the residents of Succoth began to enjoy what they called fish night, and Jesus enjoyed his reputation as a fisherman.

It was an idyllic time for the refugees from Herod, but suddenly it was over.

Jesus' fifth birthday, in Succoth, was celebrated with great pomp and ceremony for a little out-of-the-way Egyptian village. Everybody came. The four strangers had captivated the hearts of everyone, and no one had given any thought to the fact that their sojourn was temporary. When Jesus had announced on a fish night that he would be five years old day after tomorrow, party time erupted.

Food was cooked, party drinks concocted, gifts gathered, games planned. And because no one wanted to miss the party by relieving him, word was sent to Barabbas to bring the sheep in so they could be penned and he could attend. It was a great, late night when the party ended. The celebrants went home and Barabbas went out to the sheep pens to see that they were secure.

That night Gabriel appeared to Joseph. Joseph told Mary, Barabbas, and Jesus next morning that an angel had appeared in a dream. The angel said that the bad people who had been a danger to them had died, and that they should return home. It would take several days to settle affairs in Succoth, but they should be able to get on the way by this day next week. Mary, Joseph, and Barabbas were elated and excited at the idea of going home, but Jesus was of two minds on the subject.

"Did the angel say we had to go? Can't we stay here, at least till I'm grown?"

No one laughed at the boy. They knew how he had loved and appreciated living in Egypt with Barabbas and the sheep, and in Succoth with the villagers young and old.

Joseph said, "Yes, the angel was very definite: 'Take your family back to the land of Israel.'" Mary took the boy on her lap. He thought he was perhaps too big for that. She talked to him about grandparents, cousins, baby John, who was almost six, Reuben and the tentmaking shop, on and on. But the last word was, the angel sent by God said to take the family and go home. That was that.

Jesus finally nodded in acceptance, slid off his mother's lap, and moved on toward the door.

"Jesus," Barabbas's voice stopped him.

"Yeah?"

"Two things," Barabbas replied, "If you're going out to tell some friends that we're going to leave, don't say anything about what the angel said about the bad people. An angel appeared to your father in a dream and told him we had to go home. Got that?"

Jesus looked at his parents and both nodded in assent.

"Got that," he answered. "And two?"

"I'm going to need some help getting the sheep back out to pasture. Maybe you can stay four nights and we can do some fishing."

The boy's eyes lit up, and he looked at his parents again. They nodded once more.

"Yippee!" he yelled, bolting out the door in a rush.

Mary looked at Barabbas, "Thank you for cautioning him. And it will be good for him to be away while we're making ready to leave."

"You're a thoughtful man, Barabbas," added Joseph.

He then went into more detail about Gabriel's visit: same clothes, staff, positive but gentle voice, and a calming, reassuring effect in his demeanor. "It's comforting to know he knows about us—where we are, telling us what to do."

"Told you!" Mary said smugly.

"Humph," grunted Barabbas.

Joseph laughed at them.

The owner of the sheep came out to the grazing lands the day before Barabbas and Jesus were to return to Succoth, bringing with him the man who was to replace Barabbas. His name was Joseph, and Barabbas took him out and stayed with him the rest of the day, moving the sheep from place to place, letting shepherd, dog, and sheep get acquainted with each other. Joseph stayed the night with them and moved them again next morning, close in to the lakeshore, for Barabbas and Jesus were going fishing one last time.

This bit of news had been noted in Succoth, and before the fishermen had stretched out the net, Mary and her Joseph, plus several other people from Succoth, showed up to observe the operation. Barabbas and Jesus talked quietly as they folded and stored the net. Then "Come on, Mama," called Jesus. "Let's go fishing!"

It did not take much persuasion. Mary doffed her sandals, clambered over the net, and took her seat in the bow. Barabbas and Jesus pushed the boat off, climbed in, and as Barabbas began to row slowly out and around, Jesus played out the net—watching his feet. Barabbas spoke to Mary only once before they beached the boat. He turned his head and spoke softly over his shoulder, "He's a born fisherman."

Mary, watching proudly as Jesus pitched the net off the stern, thought of a remark Joseph had made: *He's a born carpenter.* She cherished those things in her heart.

This day there was no lack of help in pulling in the net, gathering up the fish, and spreading the net to dry. As some of the villagers began to clean the fish, Barabbas saw he wasn't needed in that capacity, so he started the fire and broiled enough fish to feed Joseph the shepherd for two days.

The owner of the sheep told Barabbas he was going to stay another night with the sheep and Joseph, but he would see that the boat and net got back to their proper place. With everything taken care of, the villagers having left for Succoth an hour before, Barabbas and Jesus walked down to the water's edge and stood side by side for perhaps five minutes or more, looking out across the water as if implanting in their hearts and minds forever the scenes, events, and memories of the past three years. Mary and Joseph, standing some twenty yards behind them, were keenly aware of what was flooding through their minds.

"Two good men," Joseph whispered to her, putting his arm around her waist.

"Three," she answered softly.

That fish night in Succoth was one to be remembered. The four refugees from Judea were to leave early next morning, but everyone was reluctant to go home and go to bed. After feasting until stuffed, then hours of reminiscing—Do you remember when? . . . Were we not lucky Samuel brought? . . . Hasn't Jesus grown? . . . Joseph made my table and chairs. . . . Mary nursed Mama when—on and on. No one knew it then, but these four had made such an imprint on the people of Succoth that conversations of this nature would be going on into the third generation.

Exhaustion finally caught up and the people dispersed. Joseph, carrying Jesus, and Mary, supported by Barabbas, went to their home and almost dropped in their tracks. Barabbas, being unused to sleeping in beds for three years, made his way to the hayloft in Hiram's stable.

Bright sunshine and hungry animals aroused the village, and by noon the four were packed and ready to leave. Last night had been a festive occasion, but today it was a subdued group gathered to see them off. Hiram broke the ice: He was loaded with a fairly large pack, knew he was headed home, so he threw his head back, brayed loud enough to wake the dead, and took off. This came as a welcome relief to both travelers and stay-at-homes. With cries of "farewell" and "mercy traveling" the four set out in Hiram's wake, sorry to be leaving such wonderful friends but glad to be on the way back to Palestine.

Getting such a late start, they used the same campsite they had used on the way down from Pelusium. After a full day of travel next day, this meant they would get into Pelusium about dark. Remembering Whitey's adage, "Better to arrive midmorning than at nightfall." Barabbas and Joseph discussed the timing of their arrival. The consensus was that if they arrived late and couldn't get a room, they could camp out again. Mary concurred. Tomorrow was Thursday. If no room was available, someone would leave Friday. They could get that room, spend the Sabbath in Pelusium, and leave the next day.

Still not recovered from the rigors of the night before, they were in bed and asleep before sundown, even Hiram.

Adhering to their schedule and in keeping with their predictions, they arrived in Pelusium in late afternoon. But contrary to expectations they did find rooms: Mary, Joseph, and Jesus in the inn; Barabbas in the hayloft; and Hiram in the stable.

Next morning, after breakfast the four set out on a shopping tour in order to replenish supplies—*necessary* supplies—for the trip back to Bethlehem. This presented a problem because the five of them were already loaded to the hilt with their meager possessions plus all the many gifts from their friends in Succoth. Not knowing just how they could solve this problem, they continued buying the necessities.

Later in the morning, winding their way through a bazaar, looking for clothing for the boy, loud, somewhat angry voices broke out immediately in front of them. "It's Amos!" called out Jesus to his parents. "Hey, Amos!" he called, pulling at his burnoose.

Amos stopped his vehement argument, looked down at the lad and had no idea who he was. Looking up he saw Mary, Joseph, and Barabbas grinning at him. He looked down again and he saw the wide smile on the boy's face.

"Lord love us, boy," he exclaimed, gathering Jesus in his arms. "You've grown a foot!"

All the greetings being over, Barabbas asked mildly, "What's all the argument about?"

Amos's face clouded up again, "I'm trying to buy an amulet, and this clown," glaring at the merchant, "wants to rob me!"

The merchant named a price, slapped his palm sharply on the counter, and growled, "Take it or leave it," doing some glaring of his own.

Amos groped in his purse, came out with several coins, selected three, and dropped the rest back in his purse. Slapping them down on the counter with a bang he said, "That's it. You'll get no more out of me. Take it or leave it!" The merchant gave the gathered spectators a broad, good-natured smile, and took it.

When the laughter died away, a chagrined Amos fastened the amulet around his neck and walked away with his friends, muttering under his breath, "I was robbed!"

Later, over a quick lunch, Amos learned of the predicament of his friends regarding the gifts they were packing. He had an immediate solution. He, Whitey, and Samuel had come to Pelusium last week on business for Levi. Whitey had left Amos in Pelusium to take care of some things while he and Samuel went on to Athribis on some other business. They would be back in three weeks and would then return to Jerusalem.

"Leave the stuff with me, and we'll bring it to Jerusalem when we come," he concluded.

Joseph and Barabbas shot Mary a quick look.

"Told you!" she mouthed silently.

They finished their shopping, went back to the inn and stable, and rearranged the packs. What they couldn't carry comfortably, they left in care of Amos.

The Sabbath began at sundown.

The day after the Sabbath they fed Hiram, ate breakfast with Amos, and loaded the donkey. Barabbas and Joseph shouldered their packs, and the refugees began the long trek home. It had been three years, but much of the way was familiar. Now there was no tension. They traveled by day, camped for the night, and the men felt no need to stand watch. Feeling no great urgency, they traveled about twenty miles a day and stopped midafternoon on Friday, making much of the fact that tomorrow was the Sabbath and that the next Sabbath day would be observed in the temple in Jerusalem.

That night, Gabriel appeared again with a message for Joseph. Joseph did not tell of the visit until the night of the Sabbath and after Jesus had gone to bed.

"I didn't think he should be aware of the possibility of more 'bad people,'" he said by way of explanation. "Gabriel appeared, said that Archelaus, the son of Herod, was now ruling in place of his father, and he may be a threat to Jesus. Because of this we are not to go to Jerusalem in Judea, but to Nazareth in Galilee. The old prophets have said that Jesus shall be called a Nazarene."

"Well," said Barabbas, "when he came to you in Succoth and said 'Go home,' we didn't know it meant really home, did we?"

There then arose a bit of an argument between Mary and Joseph versus Barabbas as to whether he, Barabbas, would continue on to Jerusalem alone or would he accompany the three of them to Nazareth. Barabbas finally settled the argument by saying, "The road's open for travelers, no restrictions. If I want to go to Nazareth to see my folks, who's going to stop me?" The smile on his face belied his words, but the set of his jaw didn't. "Let's count up the miles," he said.

End of discussion.

They wound up with a rough estimate of about 120 miles, six more days, up the coast by Gaza and Ashkelon and on north into Nazareth.

CHAPTER THIRTY-ONE

When the little group arrived in Nazareth, Mary was astonished and ecstatic to learn that she had a baby sister almost two years old. Needless to say, Jesus was delighted to hear that he had an Aunt Hannah, about three years younger than he. Regardless of age, he always referred to her as "my Aunt Hannah."

The grandparents and Barabbas's father and mother had last seen Jesus when he was only three or four days old, and they made much over him. The villagers knew vaguely that the four had been in Egypt; Elizabeth had told them that when she had arrived with baby John three years ago. She had gone back to Ain Karim in about six months but had never divulged the real reason for their flight with the boys.

The homecoming party was the Succoth farewell all over again, and Barabbas thought to himself, *This is getting old!* He felt he had partied out. So did the other three, and each of them looked forward to some sort of a regular routine. Jesus had already looked for and asked about a lake, and Barabbas told him about the Sea of Galilee.

"How big is it and how far?" He jumped on that information like a duck on a June bug.

Barabbas laughed at the boy's eagerness and tousled his hair in an affectionate gesture.

"It's about fifteen miles to Tiberias, a town on the coast. We can go over that way, take camping gear, and spend the night. Come back next day. Don't want to go into the city. I'll show you Mt. Tabor, too. May have to stay two nights. But don't count on any fishing. This is a sightseeing trip."

Jesus was bouncing with eagerness to go find his mother, but Barabbas reined him in. "Hold on a minute. We had better take Hiram along; you're getting too big to carry. Now, get your story straight. What are you going to ask your Mama?"

"We're going over to the Sea of Galilee, near Tiberias, and camp out. Won't be fishing and not going in the city. You're going to take me to Mt. . . ."

He looked a question at Barabbas.

"Tabor," Barabbas said.

"Take me to Mt. Tabor. Can we climb it?"

Barabbas nodded.

"And we need to take Hiram—Why? I can walk."

"We'll take him anyway, if she lets us go. Go over it again. And remember, two nights."

Jesus went over the story again, no questions, and Barabbas let him go.

The boy found Barabbas at the town well late in the afternoon, breathless from running and searching. "Babbas, we can go, day after tomorrow. That's first day of the week. And we can take Hiram. Great, what?"

"Yeah, that's great. Have Joseph—have your father get your gear together. I'll check with him later. And get to bed early the night before we go. We'll leave by sunup."

When the sun came up the two were five miles out of Nazareth, Barabbas accommodating his stride to that of the boy's, Hiram *clip-clopped* along, head bobbing, glad to be going somewhere with these two.

They were on the road that would take them south of Tiberias, a little above the south end of the lake, and before noon they could see Mt. Tabor in the distance. They stopped to rest at intervals, Jesus disdaining to suggest that he ride Hiram, and by midafternoon they were at lakeside.

At Jesus' question about fishing prospects at a later date, Barabbas told him that had best be done around Capernaum, at the north end of the lake.

"Was that where the man got his feet caught in the net?" asked Jesus.

"Yeah, in that neighborhood," answered Barabbas. "Lots of fishermen and fishing boats go out from there."

Walking up and down the lakeshore, they picked a suitable campsite, cooked and ate an early supper, and lazed around the fire. Listening to the water lapping against the shore, they quickly dropped off to sleep.

Early in the morning they were awakened by the sound of a fishing boat out on the water. Scrambling down to lakeside they were in time to see four men pull in their net with a sizeable catch. After much calling back and forth, good-natured joking and laughter, Barabbas and Jesus were broiling fish for breakfast with enough left over for another meal.

The two spent their second night at the foot of Mt. Tabor. Neither felt the urge to climb the mountain, so they lazed around again after supper. Barabbas was talking to Jesus at great length, telling him some of the history of the mountain. Pausing a moment to gather his thoughts for further discourse, he heard the steady breathing and realized the boy was asleep. Covering him against the night chill and replenishing the fire, Barabbas lay down and marveled again at how fortunate he was to have such an intimate relationship with this man-child.

Arriving back in Nazareth next day, Jesus was very voluble about the trip and obvious about emphasizing the fact that they could have left Hiram in the pasture. Barabbas was careful to refrain from mentioning how long it took to make the last five miles back to Nazareth. After all, the boy did walk the whole distance.

Barabbas began to realize he was delaying his departure from Nazareth purely for the sake of his companionship with the boy. He wanted to see Jesus grow up, start to school, mature. What kind of man would he be? A good man, no doubt, morally, physically and mentally. But how about ambition, accepting responsibility for himself and others?

All these thoughts were running through his mind next day and collided headfirst with thoughts of Reuben in Jerusalem. And Levi. And Herod, brigands. He realized his conscience had been pricking him for days.

Better start thinking about what kind of a man you are, he thought. *Reuben has been accepting his responsibilities and yours for three years. How long has it been since he's been home to Nazareth? More than four years! Thought of him lately? Wake up, man.*

Barabbas was negating the fact that for three years he had put his plans on hold and had devoted his time and efforts in securing the safety of others. But he had had such a good time doing it! That's why he was feeling such guilt. Like so many altruistic people, Barabbas sometimes felt inadequate because he didn't, or couldn't, do more. That was the kind of man he was.

Even his work with brigands—illegal, immoral, oft times violent, and certainly dangerous—was done for the good of his own people, to try to free them from the yoke of Rome.

He had fought his guilt long enough; it was time to go. He made his rounds to say goodbye and promised Reuben's parents he would send their son home for a visit. He saved Mary, Joseph, and Jesus for last. It was somewhat tearful. Mary and Joseph had known he would leave Nazareth for Jerusalem sometime, but Jesus was devastated. He had not anticipated any such thing. Life was herding sheep, camping, fishing, cooking out, listening to stories of olden heroes, of God's blessings and punishments—all this with Babbas.

"What am I going to do?" he wailed.

It took a while to mollify him. Finally, wiping his tears, he said, "I'll walk with you in the morning. Two miles," holding up two fingers.

Barabbas knelt before him. "Boy, this isn't easy for me either. Don't make it any harder than you have to. I'll feel a lot better looking back and seeing you standing here with your parents than I would to look back and see you standing alone, two miles down the road." He held up two fingers. The four of them smiled through their tears.

Next morning he looked back and saw the three of them standing a little apart from the others at the well. He stopped, turned, and waved. Turning away he stumbled on, blinded by his tears. Looking up, he murmured, "God, it couldn't get any worse than this!"

Barabbas's arrival in Jerusalem elicited as much jubilation there as it did tears and sorrow at his departure from Nazareth. Levi had a method of getting and sending messages throughout Palestine and other adjacent areas, primarily through the brigand network. He had heard of the group's departure from Pelusium and had told Reuben. He, Seth, and Judas had counted days, estimated time, and looked in vain.

Finally, after checking with Elizabeth in Ain Karim and with Joab in Bethlehem, Reuben—smart man that he was— deduced that they were on their way to Nazareth. The three counted days again, and Reuben figured Barabbas was two days late. He had not anticipated the trip to the Sea of Galilee with Jesus.

All this and more came out in two days and nights of conversation.

Joab had missed Mary, Joseph, and Jesus and had sent his boys to retrieve Joseph's tools and household goods. Barabbas saw that they were soon on their way to Nazareth via caravan.

Herod's men had later questioned Joab about what had happened to the family of three, but he had convinced them that he knew nothing. No one had ever connected them with Zechariah, Elizabeth, and baby John.

Some of Herod's men had been in the shop making inquiries about Barabbas. Levi and Reuben had expected this, and Reuben told them Levi had sent him somewhere on business. When Levi was questioned, he gave some vague and evasive answers and was rich enough and powerful enough in Jewish circles to get away with it.

So the matter of the so-called King of the Jews the wise men had been seeking faded away, and with the death of Herod, it had been forgotten.

The tentmaking business was still growing, and Reuben had hired two more men, one on deliveries and the other as a part-time tentmaker who also worked on delivery. When Barabbas came back to work, responsibilities would be shifted somewhat.

Barabbas took a week or ten days to touch base with various people and places. He visited Joab and his family in Bethlehem. Joab's wife was still seeing that the stable was cleaned regularly—three times a week. He visited Elizabeth in Ain Karim and gave her news of Mary, Joseph, and Jesus. To Barabbas, John was a strange lad: polite, smart, but somewhat of a loner. He couldn't imagine John and Jesus playing together or having common interests.

Barabbas also made contact with brigands, but not on brigand business. Levi had advised him to hold off awhile on that career. He was to get reacquainted with the men, going from cell to cell over a period of time. He began to get excited about tentmaking and fomenting trouble.

— Hiatus . . . —

The sun comes up, goes down, and days become weeks. Weeks turn into months. Then they become years, and before you know it you are an old man.

So ruminated Barabbas as he sat in the shop and plied his needle. Reuben was in a meeting with Levi, and both Seth and Judas were out with customers. So it fell Barabbas's lot to tend the shop. He had recently had a birthday and couldn't believe he was fifty-four. If Joseph had lived, he would be sixty-four.

After returning from Egypt, Mary, Joseph, and then the children always came to Jerusalem for the Passover celebration. The children stopped coming when they reached their late teens, and three years ago Mary was alone on the caravan. And last year she didn't even have Hiram; he had died.

Barabbas stashed his needle and looked at the wall across the room, seeing nothing but old friends who were gone—some having moved away, but most just dead and buried.

They began to walk through his memory. Zechariah and Elizabeth—no one knew anything about John until three years ago.

And Joab the innkeeper. Remembering him, Barabbas smiled. He wondered if his widow, Ruth, was having the grandchildren clean out the cave stable two or three times a week.

Then his and Reuben's parents and other old friends in Nazareth.

Now, several of the brigands with whom he had been closely associated. Thinking of them brought Levi to mind. "Must be in his seventies," Barabbas muttered. Jonah had said last week that Levi was talking about resigning as head of the outfit. "And what about Reuben? He's older than I am."

Barabbas was so lost in thought he was startled when the door banged open and Judas rushed in. "Guess what I just heard!" he blurted.

"The sky is falling," Barabbas answered.

Judas grinned at him as he approached. He dearly loved this man and understood his moods.

"No, but almost. The customer I just left? He's from Bethany, over beyond Jordan. Remember baby John over in

Ain Karim? About three years ago John was out in the desert, living and looking like a wild man. He came in to the Jordan, preaching, ranting and raving like crazy, baptizing people in the river. This man said Jesus came to John to be baptized. Saw John do it!"

Barabbas was taking this in without comment, tying it in with what he had been pondering over all morning. Judas thought he was having trouble recalling events and decided to help.

"You remember. John was carrying on all over the place about Herod's doings, and Herod had him put in prison. Cut his head off!"

Barabbas winced. He often thought of Judas as his son, loved him, but the boy was blunt. "Yeah, yeah, I remember. Hush a minute and let me think."

Barabbas did some mental calculations. He was twenty-one when Jesus was born. That makes Jesus thirty-three, about thirty when the customer said John baptized him. That's about when I heard of him picking some of his followers and going up, down, and all over Palestine, preaching, teaching, healing. Wonder what Mary makes of all this. Not long till Passover and she'll be here and I can ask her.

He looked at Judas. "I've been cooped up in here all morning, and you know I can't stand that. You had anything to eat?"

Judas nodded.

"Seth and Reuben should be back soon. I've got to get out and stir around a bit. I'll be back about dusky dark."

Judas nodded again and Barabbas went out through the kitchen, where he picked up a small loaf of bread and went out the back door.

CHAPTER
THIRTY-TWO

Thirty-four years ago, the actions of Barabbas had been instrumental in foiling the plans of the Demetrius-led gang of robbers. Faisel and Ahmed had walked away empty-handed, and since then Faisel had kept one purpose in mind: Get even. He had never deviated one iota.

He changed his name, his appearance, his personality, his religion, and became more Jewish than most Jews. He was smart and played his part well.

He knew Reuben and Barabbas were going to Jerusalem. About four months after his humiliation by Barabbas, he came to the city, walked the streets, loitered around the gates, and eventually spotted his quarry. It didn't take him long to learn about the tentmaking enterprise and the tenuous connection with Levi, a rich, respected Jew.

He knew he should not stay in Jerusalem until he had perfected his new character, so he chose Joppa as his base and became a merchant. Since Barabbas seemed settled in his new life, Faisel—now called Daniel—didn't worry about losing him, but went to Jerusalem twice a year to see if he was still there. Once Barabbas was gone for a long period of time, but with a few discreet inquiries he learned that he would return.

Being of the same ilk, Daniel cultivated a few underworld characters as cronies, and after a long period of time he learned of the brigands. Finally his big break came. Barabbas was a member!

Daniel knew generally what the members were doing, and he purposely began to attract attention in Joppa. If he had learned anything well in all those years, it was patience. It paid off, and as an upstanding member of the Jewish community in Joppa, quite fervent in his criticism of Roman rule, he was investigated thoroughly and became a member of a brigand cell in Joppa.

Patience, Daniel, patience! After some twenty years of building a life in Joppa, the people of that city were surprised and disappointed to learn that Daniel was moving to Jerusalem and going into a mercantile partnership there. He came well recommended in all instances. A year later the business was doing well. He bought out his partner and became a member of a brigand cell in Jerusalem.

Due to the business acumen of Reuben and the customer relationships cultivated by Barabbas, the two had become quite wealthy and were well known and honored in the business, social, and religious worlds of Jerusalem. In addition, Barabbas had risen high in the ranks of the brigands. Levi was still the titular head of the organization in Jerusalem, but Barabbas was becoming more and more instrumental in setting policy for civil disruption. He picked the time and place for hitting targets and also assigned various cells to specified projects.

One thing stuck in his craw however. Instead of being on the cutting edge, in on the action, Levi had insisted that he should not participate in any action by any cell. He was too well known and too recognizable. In fact, while such actions were in progress, Barabbas was to be somewhere with a group, which provided him with an ironclad alibi. This bothered Barabbas. He told Levi, "It's like I'm a coward, hiding behind Mama's aprons."

Levi tried to assure him this was not the case, but Barabbas was hard to convince. At any rate, he had to accede to Levi's directives.

Actually, the cells were very protective of Barabbas. They knew he had been where they now were. He had fought the battles, taken the risks, been battered and bloodied, but had never been caught. "Don't let him get in trouble now," they said.

But trouble for Barabbas was brewing in a cell out on the edge of the city. It had been brewing a long time, for almost thirty-four years.

Barabbas was in the meeting-place of that cell, near the East Gate, briefing the members on some disruptive action that was to take place in about thirty days.

There was to be a festival in the city a month before the Passover celebration. It would take place down near the temple, and there would be celebrants from all over Palestine. It was a good time for a riot, as these people would be taking the news of the insurrection back to their various home communities. This would tend to cast a pall on the feast of the Passover and would double or triple the effect of the disturbance on the Jewish community, not only in Jerusalem but all over Palestine.

"We are using you people out here because you are less likely to be recognized in the downtown area. You will be well protected by members of other cells, and once you start trouble, the riff-raff of the city are prone to jump in and add to the melee. This should be a beautiful bit of trouble, and I thank you for providing it. Your local officers will brief you on the details."

Barabbas lingered a short while, talking with ones he knew and being introduced to some he didn't know. Daniel made it a point to leave the area for a few minutes and return only when he saw Barabbas leaving.

Daniel had cultivated the friendship of an insecure, self-effacing member of this cell who was flattered with the attention of one as independent and assured as Daniel. He had also discovered the man was greedy and that money loomed large in his thinking.

About a week after the meeting when Barabbas had set up the trouble spot for the approaching festival, Daniel had whetted the man's interest and greed by hints of a mysterious stranger who would pay well for certain information.

Daniel continued to play on this theme, painting pictures of future opulence and favorable publicity for the small matter of divulging a little information. In fact, the stranger had given him, Daniel, half the money already, thirty pieces of silver, and was to give him the other half tomorrow.

"Just think," said Daniel, jingling the coins from one hand to the other, "sixty pieces of silver for a little information." The weakling named Ezra capitulated, and Daniel had him.

In truth, there was no mysterious stranger and no money had changed hands. Daniel was using his own money as bait. Having gauged his man well, he knew sixty pieces of silver, gleaming and clinking before Ezra's eyes, was more than enough to buy him body and soul.

Now he had to find the missing link in his chain, a mysterious stranger. Daniel lived and had his business near the east gate of the city. He had more than a passing acquaintance with the Roman centurion who was quartered near the west gate. This relationship, like all of Faisel-Daniel's plans, had been painstakingly built over a period of time.

In his guise as a concerned citizen, Daniel approached Centurion Anthony with some disturbing news: "I am not at liberty to divulge when or where I heard this, nor do I know if it is a civil or religious matter. Perhaps you can tell me what I should do."

"Just what is it you have heard?" Anthony asked.

"In about two weeks," Daniel answered, "at the time of the festival, there is to be a planned riot and civil disturbance in the vicinity of the temple. There will be physical mayhem and, more than likely, damage to property. As a concerned, law-abiding citizen, I feel it is my duty to let someone know."

Anthony's interest arose quickly. He was recently in a meeting with some of his superiors where the military had been thoroughly castigated by civil and religious leaders for the spate of civil unrest that had abounded lately. He, for one, was still smarting.

"And who is behind this upcoming spot of trouble?" he asked.

"That's what I can't tell you now," replied Daniel. "My life is in enough danger being here with you. I've tried to think this thing through so I can come out with a whole skin. I have a friend who can corroborate what I have told you.

"We will be at the scene of the riot. Arrest us, take us to prison, and spread the story that you put us on the rack and forced the information out of us. We will testify at the trial. For delivering this person to you and for testifying against him, we want safe conduct out of the country. . . . Is it a deal?" Faisel-Daniel looked at Anthony, no guile in his eyes, but with hate and hope in his heart.

As for Anthony, he sensed that there was more here than Faisel-Daniel was telling. Something he could not put his finger on.

When Faisel-Daniel had showed up, and began to visit with some regularity, Anthony had thought that there might be a hidden agenda. Consequently he had the man's background checked out, even back to Joppa. Nothing turned up that indicated he was other than who he said he was. And the recent criticism of the military still rankled. He made his decision. "I will have to confer with my superiors on any deal. See me in a couple of days and I'll let you know."

Two days later, Faisel-Daniel, by prearrangement, met again with Anthony. The deal was made and the trap was set.

The riot erupted as planned. Before it reached full bloom, the twenty-five soldiers in various disguises as celebrants began to throw off the outer garments that hid their uniforms, and were shouting, "Halt! Stop! Catch that man!'

Strangely enough, there was no one to catch except a few of the riff-raff Barabbas had mentioned. They knew no where to run. As the first soldier, in his eagerness to shed his disguise, dropped his helmet with a clatter, shrill whistles went up from three directions.

To a brigand this meant two things: Abort and run. Those out on the fringes did run, most just melted away into the crowd, yelling like the soldiers, "Stop him! Catch him!" as they pushed their way to the fringes, where they disappeared like wisps of smoke.

Two criminals were caught, purposely of course. Their names were Ezra and Daniel. They were rushed off to the Roman prison and supposedly put on the rack and made to talk.

Actually, Daniel and Ezra were locked up for safekeeping until the trial. For testimony against Barabbas they had been promised immunity and safe conduct to Gaza under armed guard, where they were to be put on a ship and carried to any port of their choice.

When the crowds had dispersed and the mopping-up began, a body was discovered. It proved to be that of a very prominent citizen from Caesarea who had friends in high places, both in Jerusalem and in Caesarea. He had been stabbed in the heart. Daniel had seen the opportunity and had struck.

That night, found asleep in Reuben's home, Barabbas was arrested and jailed, charged with insurrection and murder.

CHAPTER
THIRTY-THREE

Faisel had insisted that he and Ezra be treated as other prisoners were treated, locked in cells when in prison and chained when they were taken outside to the court chambers, where they were taught and rehearsed as to their testimony.

As for Barabbas, he was given no opportunity to consult a lawyer. This was one man who was going to be tried, convicted, and executed, all in short order. The chief prosecutor wanted him put on the rack and made to talk, but the centurion in charge of his guards vetoed the idea.

"I know his type," he said. "Cut off his hands, pluck out his eyes, skin him—he'll faint, but he won't talk. Nail him to a cross, not a peep out of him.

"That prisoner Ezra? Look at him hard, and he'll scream his head off! The prisoner Daniel? He's like Barabbas. He knows a lot he's not telling, and he'll lie to crucify Barabbas. But tell the whole truth? Not a chance."

The day of the trial, Faisel-Daniel related how Barabbas had met with a few people—he couldn't remember their names—and had given detailed instructions about how to start the riot, feed the flames, and disrupt the orderly progress of the festival. "Kill if you have to!"

His testimony was corroborated by Ezra. That was enough. Barabbas was sentenced to death by crucifixion, but not right away. The sentence was to be carried out during the feast of the Passover when a lot of people would be in town. Thus, the world would see how Rome meted out justice!

A contingent of five soldiers was to leave in the morning before daybreak, to take the two witnesses to Gaza, where they were to be placed in custody of the ship's captain and carried safely out of the country. For more than thirty-four years Faisel-Daniel had dreamed of gloating face to face over Barabbas. If he was going to realize that dream, it had to be done today.

At the request of Faisel-Daniel, the jailer had ordered that his chains be removed and that he be conducted to Barabbas's cell. He was disappointed when he arrived. There were two openings in the door: one at floor level, through which his meals of bread and water could be passed inside and his small bucket of human excrement could be passed out. The other opening was a small slot, barred, at what was deemed to be eye level, for the purpose of visible and vocal communication.

"Barabbas!" Faisel called.

Barabbas had seen and heard the testimony of Daniel and Ezra at the trial, and he had recognized Daniel as Faisel from that long-ago caravan. He would not have known him meeting him somewhere on the street, but as Faisel-Daniel testified, his voice took on the timbre of the threatening voice he remembered so vividly.

"Faisel," Barabbas answered. "I've been expecting you."

Faisel heard a rustle of clothing, then chains clanking as Barabbas shuffled over to the door. "What did Demetrius charge you and Ahmed for that camel and donkey you left with us that day?" he asked as he reached the door. "Tell you what. My conscience has hurt me about that. I should have paid you for those animals. I don't have any money with me," he chuckled briefly, "but if you go by the shop and see Reuben, he'll pay you. With interest," he added.

Faisel was livid. He had come to gloat, and the fool was laughing at him! He was so angry he almost turned and walked away, but he decided to stay and have the last word.

"I'll walk out of here a free man; I won't be carrying a cross like you will," he snarled. "We're leaving in the morning for Gaza, where we'll take a ship for no-one-knows where. When the Passover feast comes and you're hanging on a cross, I'll be back in business. How do you like that?"

Barabbas wanted the last word. And got it.

"Faisel," he said softly, "I'll be dead and buried—out of it. But where will you be? Do you think Reuben and my friends will forget you? You'll lock your doors and windows at night and go to bed, seeing moving shadows on the walls. You'll sit in a mosque or synagogue, looking over your shoulder. An acquaintance will touch you on the shoulder to get your attention and you'll jump and turn with a knife in your hand.

"Faisel, I had rather be in my sandals than yours."

He turned, shuffled back to his corner, put his back to the wall, and slid down to a sitting position to await his supper.

He had no hidden meaning in his last remarks to Faisel. All he wanted to do was to make his life miserable and uncertain. When he heard Faisel walk away without responding, he thought he had accomplished his purpose.

Barabbas had had no company since his arrest. He had had a speedy trial and was convicted on the testimony of Faisel-Daniel and Ezra, with his execution deferred until the time of the feast of the Passover. Since the authorities would allow him no visitors, that meant about two more weeks with no news or knowledge of what was going on in the outside world.

Levi, with all his standing and influence in the business and religious communities, could not secure visitation rights. But he was not without his resources.

For years Levi had had a confederate on the prison staff. His name was Abel. He was well educated, very smart, and a good actor. The man played the role of a retarded person, was the butt of many jokes, never showed anger, cost practically nothing in wages, served as a gofer, and picked up valued bits of information for Levi. When the guard returned from taking Faisel-Daniel to talk to Barabbas, one well-placed remark Abel made set the conversation going among the other guards present. Levi's man soon learned, almost word for word, of the entire conversation between Barabbas and Faisel-Daniel.

Having already been told to go out into the city on an errand, he had loitered about, hoping the guard would return before he had to leave. After all, no one ever expected him to be on time, considering his mental shortcomings. Getting to his feet, he created a lot of hilarity among the guards by stumbling around the room several times with the lament, "My foot's gone to sleep."

Abel soon made his exit to run his errand and, keeping in character, he went a roundabout way to make his report to the one who would pass it on to Levi. He then went by the marketplace and gave the vendor a piece of paper with the name of the item he was to bring back to the prison. Thus he fed the legend of being simple-minded.

When Levi received the report from Abel, his prison informer, he made quick contact with Jonah, who had worked for years with Barabbas in directing operations of the brigands. Levi had long considered them as co-captains of the organization in Jerusalem and its environs.

When Jonah came in, Levi met him at the door and told him of Abel's report as they walked across the room toward Levi's desk and seating area. Jonah stopped in midstride.

"That's all I need to know. I'll take care of this, and that's all you need to know." He gave Levi a quick embrace and made a hurried exit.

Within three hours Jonah, through his lieutenants, had alerted and enlisted fifty men from the several cells in the city. When the messenger had gone to the cell near the east gate and had asked the leader to select ten men for this operation, he met with quiet rebellion.

"It's all or none," the man said flatly.

The messenger understood. This cell, in their sight, had committed an unpardonable sin in accepting and harboring two such men as Daniel and Ezra, and they felt they would be a long time in redeeming themselves.

"All right," he answered. "Bring 'em all."

Jonah knew the soldiers with Daniel and Ezra would take one of two routes: the fairly well traveled main road to Gaza, or the trackless way to the south, across the desert, which would require carrying water.

He put two men near the prison to follow the company out of the city. They were to stay separated so that should one be spotted and caught the other could likely remain free. He had two more hidden farther out, one on each route. He also split his force in half, sending one half down each path, being careful to stay away from the well-traveled road and moving far south of the probable desert route. When it was determined which road the soldiers were taking, runners were to move with all possible speed to each of Jonah's forces, acquaint them with the information, and the two groups were to unite at a predetermined spot. The soldiers and both of Jonah's forces had camels loaded with water bags.

The soldiers left the prison just after midnight, and it soon became apparent that they were going the desert route. The two who were to determine this stayed on the trail until absolutely certain, then they separated, ran ahead, and reported what they had learned to the other two stationed farther out.

Jonah's forces were united before noon. By the ninth hour they had set up their ambush.

They had selected an ideal spot. The five soldiers, with Faisel-Daniel and Ezra in their midst, had just emerged from a narrow defile and gone about forty yards out into the desert again when, at the sound of a shrill whistle, twenty men literally erupted up out of the sand, forming a semicircle in front of them. At the same time, from around each of the two hills that formed the defile ten more men appeared.

Spreading out, they joined the others. Hearing a noise behind them, the centurion in charge of the contingent looked back, where ten more came out of the defile.

The centurion was a brilliant military commander. He could recognize a problem, sense a solution, make a decision, and give a command, all in short order.

Forty to fifty men, well armed. We five could kill ten, maybe, before we are overrun and killed. And for what? These two rats!

This ran through his head in seconds.

When the whistle sounded and the first group had sprung up out of the ground, Ezra yelped like a rabbit struck by a hawk and fainted dead away. Faisel-Daniel was startled, shocked, and started to run. Three of the soldiers closed in around him. Then, as he had done on the caravan with Barabbas and Reuben, he accepted what he couldn't change.

At least I got Barabbas, he thought.

"Stand fast!" the order came sharp and crisp from the centurion as his men half-drew their weapons.

"Look around you. Recognize any of these men?"

The second thought that had scuttled through the centurion's mind took another half minute. *These men aren't masked, and I recognize at least ten of them—including Reuben the tentmaker. That means we can bargain or die.*

"Do you know some of them?" he asked again.

The four looked carefully around the circle surrounding them and nodded in affirmation.

"Who is in charge of this—uh, army?" he asked pleasantly.

Jonah stepped forward. "I am," he answered.

"Ah, yes. Jonah, isn't it?"

Chapter Thirty-Three

"That is correct," Jonah answered. "And your name is Anthony."

"So you know us, and we know many of you. You don't want to kill us or you would have done so already. Have you thought of a way all of us can get out of this without being led to the executioner?"

"I think we can settle this to the mutual benefit of all of us," answered Jonah. "Shall you and I walk out and talk privately, or here, where everyone will be aware of all that's going on?"

"My men have a vital interest in this—their heads." The centurion smiled briefly. "I would like for them to hear all the details. I don't know about your men."

"My men have a vital interest also. If two so-called prisoners and five soldiers should disappear from the face of the earth, Caesar would have Palestine under lock and key for years to come and more than five heads would roll."

Jonah looked around the circle at his men, and the ones he could see nodded solemnly.

"Shall we walk around this hill, have a drink of water, and get out of the sun? You may keep your weapons, and two of my men will carry that one." Jonah pointed his chin at Ezra. "And have your men keep Faisel safe," he added.

"Faisel?" asked the centurion as they began to move. "I thought his name was Daniel."

"It's a long, long story, Anthony. And some day, when all this blows over, I would like to tell it to you."

The plans were laid out, discussed, amended, finally adjudged to be workable, and were approved. The soldiers clasped arms with Jonah and some of his men, took up the lead rope of their water-carrying camel, and set out for Gaza.

The twenty-three brigands from the east-gate cell conferred briefly with Jonah. The leader said, "We'll take them south to a place some of the men know about. And Jonah, it will be quick—no humiliation of words. Everyone has a right to die with dignity." He paused a moment, bit his lip, and looked away. "I wish Barabbas could," he said softly.

Jonah embraced him and whispered, "Make it quick." They walked away. Ezra, who appeared to be dead already, was roped to the back of a water camel.

CHAPTER THIRTY-FOUR

Two mornings later Anthony went down to the docks in Gaza looking for *The Sheba*, Captain Ahab's ship. Finding it, he went up the gangplank, saluted the sailor on watch, and asked to see Captain Ahab. Soon he was being greeted by the captain.

Anthony introduced himself, presented his credentials from the garrison in Jerusalem, and took a seat.

Captain Ahab looked over the papers. "Oh yes, the two prisoners from the prison in Jerusalem, to be delivered to an unnamed port. An unusual request. I've been expecting you. In fact, you're a day late. I was supposed to have sailed yesterday." He sounded a little peevish.

Anthony settled back in his chair a bit, took a slow look around, stood up, opened the door, and took a long look up and down the companionway. He shut the door and walked up to Captain Ahab's desk. "I'll get to the point," he said. "I expect if I inspected *The Sheba* from stem to stern, from top to bottom, I could find a dozen or so violations that would keep you in port for a month. Right?"

Captain Ahab blanched. He knew such conditions could be found if one knew where to look, and this Centurion Anthony appeared to be not only confident but competent. It was a shakedown, pure and simple. He was furious, livid, but put a tight rein on his temper.

"How much do you want?" He almost strangled on the words.

"Oh, I don't want any money," Anthony answered. "In fact, I'm going to give you some. Sixty pieces of silver." It was Ezra's payoff from Daniel that Jonah had passed on to Anthony.

He removed the silver from a pocket in his tunic and made two stacks on Ahab's desk. Ahab looked at it and back at Anthony.

"Who do I have to kill?" he asked dryly.

"Strange that you should ask that," Anthony replied. "I'll tell you what I want. That's all you need to know, and you can draw your own conclusions. I have four soldiers waiting for me on shore. We will leave this afternoon on the return trip to Jerusalem. When I get what I want from you, the five of us can't talk and you can't talk. Is it a deal?"

"What do I give you?" Ahab asked.

"You have made out a receipt for two prisoners, named Daniel and Ezra, delivered by me into your keeping?"

"I have made out the receipt, but have not written in your name."

"Date it, write in 'Centurion Anthony,' and sign it."

"That's all?" Ahab asked.

"I want another receipt. The one for the prisoners I turn in to the jailer at the prison. The other one says, 'I, Captain Ahab, of the ship *Sheba*, this day accepted sixty pieces of silver for a receipt for two prisoners delivered to my care, when I have not received two such prisoners.' Sign and date it."

"What happens to this receipt?" asked Ahab.

"I seal it up, give it to my lawyer with instructions that it be destroyed in twenty years or at my death, whichever comes first."

Captain Ahab dated, signed, and delivered the two receipts. Then he prayed to whatever god looks after unscrupulous sea captains, to make sure Centurion Anthony employed an honest lawyer.

After the soldiers left for Gaza and the east-gate brigands headed south with Faisel-Daniel and Ezra, the rest of Jonah's forces dispersed and returned to Jerusalem from every direction and at different times.

Jonah went directly to Levi to make his report. "Mission accomplished," he reported. "That's all you need to know."

"I need to know the whereabouts of the soldiers," protested Levi.

"They left yesterday afternoon for Gaza. Hopefully they will be back in Jerusalem in three or four days, with all possible leaks plugged tight."

"Good. Good," beamed Levi, rubbing his hands together in hearty approval.

"Now. There have been some other developments here we need to talk about. Barabbas has a chance!"

Jonah rose to his feet so suddenly his chair crashed over backward. "A chance? Barabbas has a chance? How in God's name can that be?"

"Calm down," urged Levi. "And pick up that chair." He smiled as Jonah replaced the upset chair and sat down again, but on the edge, leaning eagerly toward Levi.

"What's the possibility? Can we break him out?"

"No, no. Nothing like that. You know we explored that possibility early on and had to give it up. Are you familiar with this Jesus of Nazareth, the vagabond teacher, making his way up, down, and across Palestine, teaching, healing the sick and lame, giving sight to the blind, feeding thousands with a small basket of food? Creating havoc with the scribes, Pharisees, even the Sanhedrin? I seem to remember, years ago Barabbas was involved some way with a young lad, a baby really, named Jesus. Wonder if it could be the same person?"

Levi stopped talking and was staring across the room, looking at nothing, searching back through the years to people, places, and events long forgotten and faintly remembered.

Jonah slipped back into his chair, waiting for this moment of introspection to pass. He loved and revered this man with all his heart and mind, as did all those who were fortunate enough to have known him well and been the recipient of his friendship, respect, and goodwill.

In a few moments Levi visibly shook himself back to the present and looked at Jonah. "Forgive an old man his wandering back into the past. It's a failing of the aged. Where was I? Oh yes, this Jesus of Nazareth. The deeply religious," his voice took on a tone of sarcasm, "the ones who make the rules, laws, issue the edicts, and then fail to live by them, they are out to get him. He has made them look bad and they can't abide that. These religious fanatics have bounced him between the high priest, the Sanhedrin, Pilate, and any other person or group they can get to condemn him. I think he's back before Pilate now."

Levi paused a moment. "By the way, one of his own betrayed him, just as Barabbas was. And getting back to Barabbas, it's a custom to release a prisoner at the time of the Passover. Pilate will do that. It will be Jesus or Barabbas. Jesus had a huge following, but I understand most of them have deserted. When Pilate puts it up to the populace, can you drum up a crowd to call for Barabbas?"

"Indeed we can," answered Jonah. "If he's with Pilate now, hadn't I better get busy?"

"Yes. . . . Yes, get on with it," said Levi, still somewhat abstracted with the past. Jonah left in haste, looking back with concern at Levi's state of mind.

Pilate was Roman governor of Judea, and Herod was king of Judea—both serving as political appointees of Caesar. Their positions of authority were hanging by a thread, and they both knew it.

The work of Levi's and Barabbas's brigands had been very effective, and echoes of civil unrest had reverberated all the way to Rome. Brigands could indeed get rid of Herod and/or Pilate, but what they did not know was that other people were standing in line, so to speak, anxiously waiting to take the place of the deposed governor or king. Thus, they might very well swap the devil for the witch.

Neither Pilate nor Herod wanted anything to do with Jesus.

Herod could have him nailed to the highest cross in Jerusalem without a qualm, but that would please the

Sanhedrin and distress hundreds and hundreds of other people. He did not want to do either.

Pilate's quandary was different. He was a lawyer and judge and knew what a trumped-up charge was when he saw one. The charges against Jesus, in a Roman court, would have been summarily thrown out, and the ones bringing such charges would have been severely censured. However, he was well aware of the influence the Sanhedrin had in Rome, and he could not afford any more criticism from that source.

He swallowed his sense of justice, came out on the balcony, washed his hands, and gave the people a choice. But the Sanhedrin and Jonah had done their work exceedingly well. The cries of the crowd, "Give us Barabbas! Give us Barabbas! Give us Barabbas!" drowned out any hope for the release of Jesus.

Pilate gave them Barabbas.

When the envoy from Pilate arrived at the prison with the writ for the release of Barabbas, Levi, Jonah, and ten of Levi's men were waiting at the main gate. Levi was still trying to remember what was nagging at him, giving him such a cause for uneasiness.

It took about thirty minutes to get Barabbas out of his cell, free the manacles and chains, climb the stairs, and get out the door. Having been in the dark for thirty days, the sudden light blinded him, and he clasped his hands over his eyes. "Who's there? I can't see!"

His voice was hoarse, raspy, and his friends were shocked beyond belief at his appearance. He was emaciated, dirty, bearded, hair tangled, and reeked of fecal matter and prison smell.

"It's Levi, Jonah, and several other friends," Jonah answered. "You're free, and we've come to take you home."

Barabbas uncovered his eyes, still couldn't stand the light, and covered them again.

"Why am I free?" he croaked.

"Jesus of Nazareth is to be crucified in your pl—"

"Stop!" screamed Levi, suddenly remembering the Barabbas-Jesus connection.

He was too late. Barabbas fell like a stone at their feet.

CHAPTER THIRTY-FIVE

Barabbas, in bed facing the wall, finally fought his way up out of the darkness into the dim light of the oil-lit room. His first thought was of complete and utter despair.

What was it Jonah had said? "Jesus of Nazareth is to be crucified in your place?" No, No! That couldn't be.

Barabbas cried out as loud as his voice could only whisper. It caused a startled movement from the two men watching by the bedside. Hearing the noise, Barabbas rolled to his other side and tried in vain to distinguish through his tears who was there.

"Who is it?" he asked.

"It's me," Levi spoke up, "and Judas. We've been here with you since we brought you home."

"Where am I?" Barabbas asked. His eyes were closed, and his voice was still raspy.

"At my house," answered Levi. "We gave you a bath, a good bath, and burned your clothes. Tried to get some food in you, but you couldn't, or wouldn't, swallow. Think you could eat now?"

"No, I'm not hungry," he answered.

Barabbas was quiet for a few moments, then asked, "Did I hear Jonah right?"

"Yes, you did," Levi answered. "I had tried all day to recall your connection with Jesus—or even if there was one. It's a problem, growing old. It never came to mind until Jonah began to speak. I tried to stop him but couldn't. Maybe you fainting was a good thing."

"What time and what day is this?" Barabbas asked.

"Yesterday was the Sabbath. It's now about midnight," Levi answered. "Tomorrow is the first day of the week."

There was another silence for a few minutes.

"Bring me some clothes, please," Barabbas said.

"But I want to tell you about Friday," protested Levi.

"Get me some clothes and you can tell me while I'm walking the floor," he answered.

Levi looked at Judas and nodded. Judas left the room and returned shortly with several garments over his arm. "I went to your house Friday and got these while they were bathing you," he announced. He looked critically at Barabbas as he threw off the sheet and struggled to his feet, holding on to a bedpost for support.

"You'll have to eat a lot before they fit," he announced.

"Help me get this robe on, and hold on to me for a while." Barabbas said to Judas. "Start talking," said Barabbas, as he walked back and forth from wall to wall, leaning heavily on Judas.

"I don't know how much you have kept up with this man Jesus," Levi began.

"Not much," interrupted Barabbas.

"Well, he's been going up, down, and across the land, teaching, preaching, healing, raising the dead, from Caesarea Philippi to Beersheba, from the Great Sea to Gador. Two things the Sanhedrin can't abide: his popularity, and the content of his preaching and teaching. He made some very powerful enemies—Annas, Caiaphas, scribes and Pharisees, priests—everybody just about who is active in the temple. They all wanted to be rid of him. They saw him as a threat to their position of power. So they drummed up false witnesses, accused him of heresy and blasphemy—you name it, they've done it. He was passed from the Sanhedrin to Pilate to Herod, back to the Sanhedrin, back to Pilate. He didn't have a prayer of a chance.

"You won't like this, but what did we know? When Pilate asked the people 'Who shall I turn loose, Jesus or Barabbas?' I had a hundred men yelling 'Barabbas.' Bet the Sanhedrin had five hundred. He was spit on, scourged, beaten, humiliated, and Friday about the ninth hour he died on a cross!"

Levi was obviously very angry at the great injustice that had been done. Barabbas was heartsick at what he had just heard. Then he thought of Mary, Reuben, Judas, and Seth, others who had watched a baby grow to be a loving, compassionate man and suffer such an end. He was still walking, back and forth, wall to wall, now without the support of Judas.

Barabbas looked at Judas. "Bring me my sandals, please."

Judas looked nervously at Levi, who nodded again in affirmation. He returned almost immediately, and Barabbas sat down, put on his sandals, got up, and walked some more.

Levi looked at Barabbas with a discerning eye.

Chapter Thirty-Five

"You're going out," he stated.

"Yes, there's something I feel compelled to do," answered Barabbas.

"You're still a bit wobbly. You ought to eat something. How about some bread and milk?"

Barabbas shuddered, looked at Levi, and smiled. "My friend, I've been living on bread and water for weeks. I may need some food, but not bread and liquid." Levi opened his mouth to reply, but Barabbas stopped him. "Don't try to apologize. I know you are trying to help. Would Hannah have a bit of stew cooked? Not much—I can't eat much."

Levi looked at Judas. He was standing close to Barabbas, ready to support him if needed.

"She has some on the fire, keeping it warm. I smelled it when I went to get your clothes and sandals. A little bowl?"

Barabbas nodded and Judas went out.

"You're going to the site of the crucifixion?" Levi asked.

"I have to, Levi. I practically lived with and raised that boy from, say, two years old to five. I tried to teach him how to take care of himself. I loved him like he was my own. How could something like this happen to him?" It was a cry of despair.

"It's politics, pride, and jealousy," answered Levi.

Judas returned with the stew and Barabbas sat down to eat. He cleaned the bowl, and as Judas did not bring any bread, he ran his forefinger around the inside of the bowl and licked it.

"Nectar!" he said, smiling at Levi and Judas. "I didn't know I was hungry."

"More?" Levi and Judas asked in unison.

"No more," Barabbas answered. "I want to be on my way."

Going to the two who stood close by, watching anxiously, Barabbas put an arm around each one and hugged them tight to his sides. "I thank you both from the bottom of my heart. There are some things I have to do, and I'm going to see Reuben. I'll come back to see you later. All right?"

They both nodded. Barabbas tightened his arms around them again, released them, and let himself quietly out the door.

"Follow him," whispered Levi to Judas, "but don't let him see you." Judas ran quickly out the back door, around the house, and spotted Barabbas disappearing into the darkness.

Barabbas had one aim in mind: He had to get to the site of the crucifixion. He had to see where the tragic miscarriage of justice had taken place.

He had walked twenty minutes and was halfway there when he heard his name called. "Barabbas?"

Barabbas stopped, stock still, one foot in suspension, waiting. He thought he was going to faint again. He had heard that voice call his name too many times to fail to recognize it now. He lowered the suspended foot slowly to the ground and turned even more slowly. There was Mary moving hesitantly toward him.

"I thought I recognized that walk. Barabbas, I'm so glad to see you!"

Mary ran toward him, arms outstretched, and threw herself convulsively against him.

Barabbas flinched. He wasn't expecting this embrace but rather recriminations. Not knowing what else to do, he put his arms around her shaking body, having to support her to keep her from falling.

The sobbing and shaking gradually subsided, and she pushed away to look up at him.

"Barabbas, I tried and tried to get in to see you, but the guards wouldn't let me in. Reuben went over and tried to bribe them, but that didn't work either. I was going to Levi and see what he could do for me, but Judas said even he couldn't get in. Whatever became of that scoundrel, Faisel? . . . Barabbas, you're thin! Was it bad, in prison?"

"Not as bad as being crucified!" Barabbas answered bitterly.

Mary held on to his arms but pushed him farther away so she could see him more clearly. "Oh, Barabbas. You poor, dear man. You feel guilty, don't you? You think you should have been hanging there instead of Jesus. I looked for you there in all that mob but didn't find you. Where were you? Didn't they release you early Friday morning? Reuben was with me, but I needed you. Barabbas, where were you?" It was a wail of hopelessness and with more sobs and shaking she hung onto him again.

Barabbas waited until she was more composed and began to explain. "Yes, I was released early Friday morning. Levi, Jonah, and several others were at the gate waiting for me. When I asked why I had been freed, Jonah said it was because Jesus of Nazareth was being crucified in my place. When I heard that, I fainted. Hadn't had much to eat or drink and I was pretty much done in. They took me to Levi's, cleaned me up, except for the stench in my nostrils—don't think I'll ever get rid of that—and put me to bed. I didn't come to my senses until about two hours ago. I've had some food and feel much better, and I've got—uh . . . um, some errands to run. Then I'll go back to Levi's."

"You're on your way to Golgotha, aren't you?"

Barabbas nodded.

"I would go with you, but I and some more of the women are going to the tomb to prepare Jesus for burial. I didn't have time to do it Friday, couldn't get anybody to help me."

"Before you go, tell me two things. Where did you come from awhile ago when you called my name?"

"Right there," she pointed with her chin to the door of a house. "I live there now. Been there since late winter." She added, "What's the other thing?"

"You always said, 'God wouldn't put me in this situation and leave me no out.' Where's your out? Gabriel directed us from time to time. Where was Gabriel? Where was God? You said you needed me. If I hadn't been in prison, if I had been here, what could I have done? Every brigand in all of Palestine couldn't have kept him off that cross."

"Mary," Barabbas put his hands on her shoulders and shook her, not very gently either. "Mary," he repeated, "the boy's dead!" It was a cry of heartbreak and anguish. "What are we going to do?" he whispered.

Mary thought she had cried herself dry. First, for Barabbas when he was arrested and then imprisoned. Then at Jesus' arrest, his beatings, his crown of thorns, his complete humiliation, the desertion of his followers, the nails in his hands and feet. And now Barabbas again. The hopelessness in his eyes and voice brought up more tears.

I'm going to be late, she thought. *But I can't leave Barabbas like this.*

"Barabbas," she said. "The man's dead, not the boy. I know you've been out of touch with Jesus for years; Judas and Reuben told me so. You have heard only a smattering of what he has been doing.

"Soon after his thirtieth birthday Jesus left home, picked twelve men as his disciples, and through them he set out to establish a heavenly kingdom, the Kingdom of God, here on earth. One of the disciples, Judas Iscariot, was like you and your brigands: He wanted an earthly kingdom. And as Faisel did to you, he betrayed Jesus.

"Barabbas, Jesus wasn't born to sit on a throne, in a palace, and rule by laws and edicts. He was born to live in the hearts of people and rule by love, in everyone and for everyone.

"I haven't slept since Jesus died. I sat up all day yesterday and last night, reliving Gabriel's visit to me in Nazareth, and the birth of that baby. Remember the stories the shepherds told us? And for the first time, last night, the reason for his birth became clear. You said all the brigands in Palestine could not have kept him off that cross. Barabbas, all the angels in heaven couldn't have either. Don't you see? He was born to die.

"Barabbas, listen to me. Listen with your heart, not your mind. You asked, 'Where was God?' I didn't know where God was, at first. Then I saw Gabriel. He didn't look at me. He was looking at Jesus, there on the cross—your cross. On his face was an expression of anguish and pity, hopelessness and despair, such as you have on your face now. He was suffering with Jesus, just as I was and just as you are. But there was something else, as if this was meant to be. And it's not over.

"It was then that I felt the presence of God. I didn't see Him, but He was there! It was as if He was saying, 'You've done your part, now I'll do Mine.' I couldn't take my eyes off Gabriel. He was tight as a drum. And when Jesus died, I was not looking at him, but I heard—you could tell it was his last breath. Barabbas, when Jesus died Gabriel let out a long breath, relaxed, and smiled. Like 'Now, that's over!' Then Barabbas, he looked at me—his eyes clear, alert, not a tear— and he disappeared in the crowd.

"Don't ask me what it means. Don't ask me what's going on. I don't know. But God didn't ask me to have Jesus, let him grow up to be a man, then die a horrible death on a cross, and stay dead. You hear that, my old friend? I don't know where, when, or how, but he can't stay *dead*! Barabbas, the Son of God may have been born to die, but he won't stay dead. Not God's Son!"

Barabbas had tried to listen to Mary's discourse with his heart, not his head. It was difficult—he was too logical. But somehow he was comforted. Mary had always had faith, had known that God had asked her to have this baby for a purpose, and that without Joseph, Barabbas, Levi, or Whitey, without any circumstance or doubt, that purpose would be fulfilled. The little seed of faith Mary had just planted was beginning to stir in its hard shell.

"Barabbas," she shook him gently. "I told you, but you didn't hear. I've got to go. I'm way late. Get in touch with me as soon as you can. Believe me, it's not over."

She hurried away.

CHAPTER
THIRTY-SIX

Barabbas stood lost in thought for a few moments, then raised his head, looked back in the direction he came from, and called, "Judas?"

It took a minute or two. Judas finally stepped out from a shadowed doorway where he had darted when Barabbas had looked back after Mary called.

"Come up here," Barabbas said, no rancor in his voice.

As Judas approached, Barabbas asked, "Levi told you to follow me?"

Judas nodded in assent.

"Why?"

"You're weak as a kitten. He's afraid—we both are—something might happen to you. You faint again, who's going to look after you? 'Specially out here this time of morning?"

Barabbas was reminded again of the faithful support, friendship, and love these two and others had shown him through the years. *How long has it been? How old is this boy?* Barabbas smiled at his thinking. *Anyone younger than he was a boy. Let's see, he was about sixteen when he came to work for us. About thirty, thirty-two years ago? Great day! The man's forty-eight, forty-nine years old.*

Barabbas put an arm around Judas's shoulders. "Judas, forgive me if I seem ungrateful. But I'm all right, really. I'll get some breakfast when I get to Reuben's. I'll eat like a horse, even get fat!" He patted his stomach. "Follow me if you want to, but there's no need," he continued. "I've got to go to Golgotha and see those crosses. I need to do that alone. Can you understand that?"

Judas nodded. "I understand. I'd have to do the same. I can feel your arm, body against mine. You're not shaking like you was at Levi's. Go on, do what you have to do, but get something to eat soon. I'll not follow. Think I had better go to the shop and report to Reuben, Seth, and the others. Shall I tell them where you've gone?"

"No, don't do that. Just tell Reuben I've got to get away for a while, think things out. He'll understand. And thank you again, my friend, for your care. I love you like a brother."

The two embraced and went their separate ways.

Barabbas had always had the gift of almost total recall of discourse or even idle conversation. As he resumed his way toward Golgotha, the words of Mary were ringing in his ears. *Barabbas, he was born to die,* she had said. And later, *When Jesus died, Gabriel let out a long breath, relaxed and smiled, like, "Now, that's over."*

The fact was, Gabriel had always taken measures to keep Jesus alive: Take the child and go to Egypt, don't go back to Judea, go instead to Nazareth.

Then why would he be relieved when Jesus died? Barabbas's mind was still dealing in logic, but logic tempered with faith. Mary had said, *Barabbas, the Son of God may have been born to die, but he won't stay dead. Not God's Son.* Mary's words went through his head like a peal of thunder. He stopped in his tracks.

"That's it," he whispered. "He'll live again!"

The seed of faith Mary had planted in his heart not only stirred, it came to full bloom. Barabbas started walking again, faster now, but stopped a second time for a moment or two when he saw the site of the crucifixion.

It was still dark, but the three crosses were silhouetted against the starlit sky. In his mind's eye Barabbas pictured the three bodies hanging there, limp and lifeless now, after having been drawn tight as a bowstring for hours, fighting against the agony of pain and suffering. It was an ugly, brutal illustration of man's inhumanity to man. Barabbas shivered in the warm gentle breeze that blew across the hill.

"No wonder Gabriel was relieved when it was over. No one should have to see friend or foe nailed to a cross."

Barabbas was at the foot of the cross, looking up. His head hurt from the crown of thorns pressed down on his brow, blood was running in rivulets across his face and down his neck. The pain from the nails in his hands and feet was unbearable. His thirst was agonizing, his tongue as big as his fist. He prayed to die, almost willed it, and dropped to his knees at the foot of the cross, leaning his brow against the rough wood.

God in heaven, he prayed in his mind, *I see it now. He was born to die, and he will live again.*

"Babbas!"

Barabbas's body jerked so suddenly his head banged against the rough wood of the cross. His hands, holding the upright, gripped convulsively and broke the cover of clotted blood that had gathered there, so that his hands were sticky. His first thought was to hope Judas had followed him. He was going to die here.

He did not recognize the voice, but he knew who spoke. No one else had ever called him by that name.

"He is alive," he whispered, "and here."

He felt a presence near and looked up. The man, Jesus, was dressed in a white robe and had a white towel in his hand.

"Here," Jesus said, handing him the towel. "Wipe your hands and come over and sit with me. I have a little time before I have to meet the women at the tomb."

Jesus walked over, sat down on a bench that had been left there after the crucifixion, and crossed his ankles. His feet were bare. Barabbas followed tentatively, wiping his hands with the towel. When he handed it back to Jesus, his hands were no longer sticky but the towel was clean.

He noticed the nail prints in the bare feet of Jesus and sat down gingerly, leaving some space between the two.

"Jesus," he tried to say, "I've . . ."

He stopped. His voice had squeaked and was unnaturally high-pitched. He cleared his throat and tried again. It wasn't any better.

"Babbas, you're uncomfortable and don't know what to say or how to say it. Take a deep breath. Try to relax. I'm the boy you helped raise, remember? Take your time."

His third attempt went better.

"Mary told me tonight what you were doing with your twelve disciples. Judas told me of some of the miracles you have done, and I've heard bits and pieces from other sources.

"Jesus, I've been so wrong, so blind. I wanted to put you, or somebody, on a throne to rule in place of Herod. As Mary said awhile ago, to rule by making laws and issuing edicts. I've spent my life trying to disrupt civil government in order to bring that about.

"That, in itself, is enough to condemn me. But I've done far worse. Until the last half-hour, at the foot of yonder cross, I've never accepted you for what you are and who you are.

"I knew about Gabriel's visit and conversation with Mary and the message from God. But I just couldn't believe God could and would do what Gabriel said. That is my worst sin: the sin of unbelief. Can you and God forgive me for that?"

"Babbas, that's dumb!"

Barabbas had been looking down at the ground when he made his confession of unbelief, unable to look Jesus in the face. The remark, "Babbas, that's dumb," startled him, but not so much that he failed to remember a night by a fire on the sheep pastures near Succoth in Egypt, twenty-five, maybe thirty years ago. Even in the dark he had seen the impish grin on the boy's face.

Now, for the first time, he looked fully into the face of Jesus the man. What he saw was not an impish grin, but a look so full of love, compassion, understanding, and forgiveness that his heart welled up within him and tears trickled down his cheeks.

"Babbas, I said awhile ago, I'm the boy you helped raise. Since I left home, three years ago, I haven't had a place to lay my head. My disciples and I have walked the highways and byways of Palestine from end to end, time and time again. We have caught fish from lakes and streams and cooked them over open fires.

"In my teaching, I have referred to sheep and shepherds, oxen in ditches, sowing and reaping. I have thought of you so many times and thanked you in my heart for teaching me and helping prepare me for what I was sent to do.

"Remember the sign you showed me down in Egypt, the one to use if I was in danger and needed help? There were times when I would have been roughed up, beaten, or maybe even stoned. I made the sign and a few men appeared, surrounded me, and led me through the mob to safety. They made no threats, just looked the crowd in the eye and walked us through. My disciples said among themselves, 'The angels take care of him,' but I thanked you and your brigands for that.

"Babbas, since that time when I was twelve and my parents went a day's journey back toward Nazareth without me, I have thanked the Father every day for bringing you into my life. My parents were frantic, looking for me all over Jerusalem, and you told them I was in the temple.

"You were misled in your work with the brigands, but what you believed in you did well. Your logic got in your way—a failing many people have."

Jesus paused a moment, looking off into the distance. "You should meet my disciple, Peter," he said, more to himself than to Barabbas.

He returned to his former train of thought. "It's not necessary, Babbas, but if you need to hear the words, we forgive you. And thank you again for what you have done for me and meant to me. I was a very fortunate boy.

"Now I must go and meet the women at the tomb."

"Just a moment; one other question." Barabbas was getting bolder, more at ease. "Mary said you were born to die. That's the part I don't understand. Why? Why?"

"Babbas, that's a long story. God the Father, I, and the Holy Spirit are one yet separate. When I ascend to the Father, the Spirit will come; and when you and others receive Him, you will begin to understand. It's a matter of faith.

"To answer your question, briefly it's this: The Jews are God's chosen people. For hundreds and hundreds of years He has blessed them and led them and they keep falling away into their own sinful ways. God punishes them, brings them back, then they fall away again.

"God's plan is that I should be born of the virgin Mary, grow up, and die on a cross for the sins of the world, for Jews, Romans, Greeks, even Persians—everyone who believes.

"I think the plan can be summed up in a lesson I taught my disciples: For God so loved the world that He gave His one and only Son, that whoever believes in him shall not perish but have eternal life." Jesus arose, stepped in front of Barabbas and placed his hands on Barabbas's bowed head as a blessing and a benediction. Then he was gone.

An hour passed and dawn was breaking before Barabbas felt inclined to move. He finally rose to his feet, stretched his arms, did some knee bends, and loosened up his body as best he could. Then he began a slow walk back into the city.

Foremost in his mind was the fact that Jesus was alive. And added to that was the joy and relief he felt deep in his heart and soul that he had reached that conclusion even before Jesus spoke to him.

"I was so blind," he muttered, "and for so long. But thanks be to God, and to Mary, I saw the light!" He laughed joyously and stepped up his pace.

Walking along with joy in his heart and a spring in his step, Barabbas came to a halt in front of the temple gates before he realized where he was. This meant he had just passed the tentmaking shop two or three minutes ago. Retracing his steps he came to the alley, turned in, and walked toward the back door. As he walked, he thought back to the time he and Reuben had rented the place from Levi thirty-four years ago. Levi had given them a deed to the property two years ago.

"You've paid for it three times," he had said. "Reckon I may as well give it to you."

Barabbas tried the door, found it locked, and knocked. The scent of cooking food reminded him he was ravenous.

Reuben fumbled with the lock, opened the door, gasped, and dropped the pot of hot food he was holding. "Merciful God, man, why didn't you give me some kind of warning?" He swarmed over Barabbas like bees over a fig bush, hugging, pummeling, patting; he couldn't keep his hands off him. Barabbas finally had to back off out of reach.

"I thought I might come in here and get something to eat," he muttered, "but it looks like you've thrown it out."

Reuben looked down; "Step over the mess and come on in. We'll start over," he grunted. "Sit down and talk to me. Do you know I haven't heard from you since the soldiers picked you up? I saw you at the trial but couldn't get close. Sit down, man, and talk to me."

Reuben turned back to the cooking area, selected a larger pot, and started over—chattering away, not really knowing what he was doing or saying. Barabbas sat, watched, and listened, waiting for him to run down. Reuben finally stopped talking, turned and looked at Barabbas, set the pot down carefully, and walked toward where he was seated. Barabbas arose from the chair, met him halfway, and they stood for minutes, arms clasped and wetting each other's shoulders with tears.

They finally released each other, stepped back, and each one, unashamed of this show of emotion, took a cloth from his belt and wiped the tears from his eyes and face.

Reuben turned again to his food preparation, looked over his shoulders at Barabbas, and said, "From the beginning."

Barabbas began with his arrest and being carried to the prison. He recounted how the jailer wanted to put him on the rack and extract a confession, and how the centurion, Anthony, would not permit it.

He told of being shackled hand and foot, locked in a windowless cell and fed bread and water once a day. He said he wondered what time of day or night it was, even what day of the week. He told of the trial, which Reuben had seen and heard, of his sentence to death by crucifixion, of days—or nights—blurring into days and nights, never knowing what the next minute might bring. He told of Faisel's visit, their conversation, and how he had responded. He at last told of his release, how he had fainted at Jonah's declaration that Jesus of Nazareth had died "on my cross."

By this time Reuben had cooked and brought their breakfast to the table and they had begun to eat.

"Reuben, I was completely wiped out at that news. Neither you nor Mary and Joseph could comprehend what that boy meant to me. As a man, it has been almost as if we never knew each other. I think we have purposely avoided each other, as if, in his wisdom, God has kept us apart. Oh, I have heard what he has been doing; Judas brought both you and me glowing reports of miracle after miracle he has performed. And I have seen, here in Jerusalem and throughout Palestine, the huge crowds following him. But it is as a boy that I have remembered him. And to think of that boy grown into a man hanging on my cross, dying in my place. Reuben, I couldn't stand it. I wanted to die."

Barabbas was weeping again.

"I understand," said Reuben, nodding his head.

"No, you don't, my friend. Not yet. I hope—I think you will when you hear the whole story. Be patient with me. Let me get my thoughts together. This is a story that must be told, but it's new to me and I want to tell it right, make it clear."

Barabbas considered for a moment. "What do you recall about Jesus' birth?"

"I know you told me about Gabriel, a so-called angel, talking to Mary in Nazareth, telling her she is to be the mother of God's Son. I know you told me about the shepherds visiting that night of his birth, and the stories they told. I know about the so-called angel telling Joseph to take Mary and Jesus and get away to Egypt. I've felt like you did; this is all too unthinkable. Don't seem possible. Like you, I've taken this with a large pinch of salt. Sounds like a miracle to me, and that's hard to believe."

Barabbas heard this declaration of doubt with fear and dread.

Dear God in heaven, he prayed silently, *don't let me lose this friend now. God forgive my unbelief.*

Barabbas looked at Reuben, an expression of love and hope in his eyes and on his face. He leaned across the table toward him. "Listen to me, Reuben. I've confessed my sins to

God and begged forgiveness. Now I confess my sin against you and ask your forgiveness. Listen to me!"

Barabbas then related how he had regained consciousness at Levi's house, eaten, dressed, and gone on his way to Golgotha. How Mary had called to him and how her declaration of faith in a living Jesus had comforted him and changed his despair to faith and hope.

"Reuben, you said you understood my feelings about Jesus. You don't—you can't until you, in your mind and heart, kneel at the foot of the cross, look up, and know that he died there for you, for me, and those who come after us, who accept that gift of grace from God our Father. That's why he died, and that's why he lives again."

"You say he's alive?" Reuben asked. "I saw him die! I saw them take him down from the cross, man. He was limp as a rag—dead weight. And I mean *dead*!"

What Barabbas had feared was what had happened. Without putting it into words, the skepticism and doubt Barabbas had felt all those years had rubbed off on Reuben. Even as children in Nazareth, in spite of being older and more mature, Reuben and others were prone to accept Barabbas as leader. So what Barabbas thought, Reuben unconsciously picked up.

Yet Barabbas was now different from the man the soldiers had taken from his home thirty or thirty-one days ago. He had a glow, an assurance, a joy Reuben had not seen.

"Did you touch him?" he asked.

"Yes, I touched him. I was kneeling at the cross, and he gave me a towel to wipe my hands. Later, he placed his hands on my head and blessed me. He said the women were going to the tomb. That's where Mary was going, to prepare his body for burial—and he had to meet them there. Reuben, I haven't seen it yet, but that tomb is *empty*! I know he is alive."

Reuben had been seeking assurance, but he still had not found it. He jumped to his feet, paced the floor, and asked, "Barabbas, what are you trying to do to me?"

"I'm trying to lead you to Jesus, but I don't know how. God, help me." It was a cry of desperation.

"Reuben, I've never talked aloud to God with anybody in my life. Will you listen with me now while I try?" Reuben looked at his friend, sat down, reached across the table, took his hand, and bowed his head.

For the first time in his life Barabbas talked aloud with his God. "Like I was with Jesus awhile ago, I don't know what to say or how to say it. I thought I had cleansed my soul at the foot of that cross, but I can't leave here, I can't die, with this friend's blood on my head. Whatever it takes, Father, make him know that Jesus died for us and that he lives again. What you have given to me, give to him. I can't think of any more words to say."

Barabbas raised his head and looked at Reuben. Reuben was looking at him with a smile on his face and tears streaming down his cheeks. "He's alive, Barabbas. I felt him near me. He was dead—*dead*! But he's alive."

Barabbas found three more words to say: "Thank you, Father."

There was silence in the room for a long time as each considered in his own heart and mind the miracle of answered prayer.

Later, they both heard noises from out in the shop, and Reuben went out to see if he was needed. He soon returned saying, "Everybody's in and working except Judas. Wonder where he is." He considered for a moment, shook his head, and sat down again.

"Barabbas, what are we going to do? What about the brigands? Where does all this leave you and them?"

"I'm through. I can't be a part of that anymore. It was all wrong anyway. We were looking for a crowned king; a king like David, Solomon. Jesus is king, but not that kind of king. He came to rule the hearts of men, not governments. He rules with love, not swords. I think Levi sees that we are through. And after what has happened, I can't stay in Jerusalem. I was tried and convicted of insurrection and murder. Jerusalem will never forget that. I have no future here. I'm going to disappear for a while, I've got to be alone and think things out."

Reuben nodded. "Will you need a backpack? Food? What about clothes? Spare sandals?"

"All of that. I may be gone awhile. I'm going out and walk around a bit. May go and see Levi. The way I look, no one will recognize Barabbas the tentmaker. I doubt they'll recognize Barabbas the murderer." He smiled sourly. "I'll be back for supper. Can you feed me again?"

"For what you've given me this day, Barabbas, I would give you my life."

"Give it to Jesus," Barabbas said as he turned toward the door.

"Already have," Reuben answered, face aglow.

When Barabbas returned about dusk, Reuben had prepared enough food, he thought, for his old friend to carry a two-day supply with him when he left. What Reuben didn't eat, Barabbas did.

Bless his heart, he's hollow, thought Reuben. "Will you stay the night?" he asked.

"Yes, I will. I'm tired. Haven't been stirring around much lately." He gave Reuben a rueful smile. "Did Judas show up?"

"No, he didn't, and that's not like him," Reuben answered. "Maybe he went back to Levi's."

"I went to see Levi. Saw several of the others, but he hasn't seen Judas. Levi had set up a meeting. Said he thought the brigands were through, at least in Palestine. Said he was getting too old to be director. Resigned and asked us, 'Who wants to take my place?' No one spoke up, so I suppose that's it. No more cells. I'm glad. I think the rest of 'em are too. Whatever made us think we could run Rome out of Palestine anyway? We must have been crazy!"

"The spirit of youth, Barabbas, the spirit of youth. The young think they are going to live forever. The sword hasn't been made that can cleave their heads. You remember how we felt."

"That was a hundred years ago. How could I remember?" Barabbas stood, sighed, and stretched. "I've got to go to bed. It's been a long day and I'm dead." He shambled off, turned, looked back, and said, "But Jesus is alive!"

He left the room.

CHAPTER
THIRTY-SEVEN

Barabbas left Reuben next morning soon after sunup. He had eaten a big breakfast. Reuben thought he was still hollow.

He loaded his backpack with supplies, selected a favorite staff, and told Reuben, "I don't know where I'm going, what I'm going to do, or when I'll be back. When I find out, I promise, you'll be the first to know. Tell Mary and Levi but no one else. I'm not looking for companionship, but for answers. You understand, don't you?"

Reuben nodded, embraced him, handed him a waist pack of fruit and nuts, and turned away, ostensibly busy at something. He didn't want to see Barabbas leave.

Barabbas left quietly, went out the east gate of the city, and continued east toward the Jordan. As of now, he had no destination in mind and was in no hurry, but neither did he tarry. To people he met, he seemed like a man with a purpose and didn't encourage any pleasantries or conversation.

Next day, he came to the shore of the Dead Sea, turned north, and now became interested in the countryside he was traversing. He had never been here before and began to slow his pace, linger a bit.

Days passed and he was still moving north on the west side of the Jordan. On an impulse, he looked for and found a crossing and continued north on Jordan's east side.

Two or three Sabbaths came and went, and Barabbas kept moving, smiling to himself as he thought of the ox-in-the-ditch incident. In fact, all this time, he had been reliving his life: growing up in Nazareth with Reuben, Joseph, Mary, and his sisters; joining with the brigands to change the world. Vivid in his mind was his picture of Gabriel's visit with Mary and his reaction to her recital of what it meant. *The regret of my life*, thought Barabbas. *Why couldn't I believe?*

Barabbas began to recognize familiar territory and realized he was nearing the Sea of Galilee. He was still on the east side of the Jordan and it was late afternoon. He began to feel some excitement stirring within.

"I'll cross the river tomorrow, go on north, and find the spot where Jesus and I camped. Bet the place hasn't changed much. Maybe there I can find some answers."

He found his answers that night.

He picked his campsite, made everything ready, took his net, and went fishing. He caught four good-sized fish and soon had them broiling over his fire. That's when, to his dismay, he heard footsteps approaching. This night he had really wanted to be alone. Ever wary and alert, he put his hand on his staff, shifted his feet and body so he could move quickly, and waited.

Chapter Thirty-Seven

Gabriel appeared out of the darkness into the firelight.

Barabbas released his staff, rose in one motion, bowed his head courteously, and asked, "Why am I not greatly surprised to see you?"

Gabriel laughed heartily and answered, "Wishful thinking, I would guess. You want answers. I think your questions started with me, up here in Galilee. So subconsciously you've come up here for answers. Are we going to let those fish burn?"

"No, there are two each, with some bread and spring water. Pull up a rock and join me."

Barabbas had been observing Gabriel very closely; it was the same man he had seen talking to Mary at the well in Nazareth over thirty years ago. The same description given by Joseph in Nazareth, in Ain Karim and in Egypt, years apart.

Well, thought Barabbas, *I guess angels don't age.*

Gabriel, meantime, was making his assessment of Barabbas. *He's older, some gray in his hair and beard. Lines in his face. But still in good condition. And not as tight; more serene, calm, not looking for trouble. Well able to take care of any should it arise, but he's not the aggressor. A good, different man. The man I expected.*

Barabbas broke the silence. "Gabriel, I was thinking of you yesterday, maybe this morning, regretting the fact that I didn't believe you, believe in you. I've wanted to apologize and tell you I'm sorry. I wasted a lot of time mulling over Mary's pregnancy, wondering about the power of God—not belittling His power, not doubting even, but just not believing He would do this.

"For what? I don't know how much you know. I don't know if you've talked to Jesus lately, or God. But a man can learn a lot at the foot of the cross. Especially if he's talking to a risen Savior.

"God, I believe, has used me for His purpose in spite of my unbelief. I've done my best with what I had. I'm ready to do better now with what He's just given me: a firm belief in the purpose and power of God. Which brings me to my first question—perhaps my only question. You do not appear to people willy-nilly, for no reason. Gabriel, what do you want of me?"

Gabriel had been listening to Barabbas with amazement and delight at his clear explanation and the concept of his journey from darkness to light. *The Father has picked the right man*, he thought. He paused and looked up with a silent prayer in his heart: *Forgive me, Father. How could you not pick the right man!*

Gabriel finished his meal, as did Barabbas, wiped his fingers with a cloth, put it away, placed some more wood on the fire, took a deep breath, and spoke: "I like the way you get to the point. I like the way you are clearing your conscience. I like the way you affirm your faith in the purpose and power of God. In fact, I like everything about you. You take what you believe in—be it good or bad—and see it through to the end. Barabbas, you are a good man, and I, an angel from heaven, sent by God, love you."

Barabbas blinked, his eyes glistened, and a tear ran down each cheek.

"And?"

"You are to go to Damascus and work and live with Judas—" at the involuntary start of Barabbas, Gabriel nodded and continued. "Yes, your Judas. He's already there. A tentmaking place became available, Judas heard of it, investigated, and acquired it. You are to work with him and wait. I don't know for how long.

"There is a man appearing on the horizon who can do great things for God. Right now, as you were, he's being misled. And like you, it's going to take something dramatic, traumatic, to turn him around. You will recognize him when he shows up. You will be with him three years, he will know when he's ready to go.

"Barabbas, he will be hungry, starving to learn about Jesus. And he's going to be living a rigorous life. You can teach him about both. You spent three years with Jesus and did him a world of good. You can do the same with this man. Can you do this?"

"As the Lord wills," answered Barabbas. "I'll do my best. How old is this man?"

"He's no babe in the woods," replied Gabriel. "He will be nearing forty. He's a brilliant man, well educated. But two things he knows nothing about: Jesus and broiling fish over an open fire. Three things: tentmaking. Teach him that, too."

Barabbas had one other question. He was thinking of his plan to cross the river tomorrow, go toward Tiberias, and find that old campsite.

"You know about my bringing Jesus over to the Sea of Galilee, camping there and at Mt. Tabor?"

Gabriel nodded.

"When do I need to be in Damascus?"

"Not right away. Your man hasn't yet begun what he thinks is his work. You want to cross over and camp—do so. But don't delay for long."

Gabriel yawned, stretched, grunted, and put more wood on the fire. "If you don't mind, I'd like to stay the night," he said.

"Pull up another rock," Barabbas answered with a chuckle.

When he awoke the next morning, the fire was burning brightly, but Gabriel was gone. Barabbas made his breakfast, giving some thought to his plan to cross the river for one or two nights. By the time he had eaten, cleaned up, and packed up, the idea of crossing the river and finding the old campsite for two nights seemed less and less attractive.

"Admit it," he told self, "you want to get on with the work at Damascus." He grinned and shouldered his pack.

He was now about halfway between Jerusalem and Damascus. It would be much more expedient to go on to Damascus from here, but he had promised Reuben he would report to him. He had to make some disposition of his share of the tentmaking business. He had to let Levi and Jonah know where he was going. Jesus had asked his disciple John to care for Mary. That would take some looking into. He started south at a trot.

It took him five days to get back to Jerusalem, and one of them was a Sabbath. His ox was beginning to prey on his conscience!

Reuben was delighted to see him again, glad to hear the news of Judas's whereabouts, and very pleased that Gabriel had provided a spot for Barabbas to be useful.

"Reuben, what are we going to do about this business?" Barabbas asked.

"Been thinking about it a little while you were gone," he replied. "The fellows working here are good people and very capable. They have already asked about the possibility of buying. Me? I'm ready to quit. Been in here over thirty years. I can go to the temple courtyard or hang around a city gate and tell lies with the best of 'em. I believe I'll enjoy that." He looked off into the distance, as if living such an existence already, and Barabbas saw a smile spread over his face.

He's earned it, Barabbas thought.

Reuben came back to the present. "What about you? This will be right much money. You going to carry it to Damascus?"

"What does an old bachelor like me need with money? Parents dead. Sisters doing all right; never see or hear from them anyway. Yeah, I'll take enough to Damascus to pay Judas out of debt. Been wanting to do something for that boy. Don't know what I'll do with the rest."

Reuben looked at him. "You hear about Jesus on the cross, putting Mary into his disciple John's care?"

"Yeah, I heard that from Levi. Why?"

"Those fellows, twelve of them, left whatever they were doing for a living and followed Jesus all over Palestine for three years. Some happened to be rich but gave their money away. One of 'em, the one that betrayed Jesus, is dead, but I'll bet the rest are poor as dirt. Why don't you look into that?"

Barabbas jumped to his feet, slapped Reuben on the back, and walked around the room in his excitement.

"What a great idea. I would never have thought of that. Thank you, old buddy. Let's go see Levi and get him to help us work this out."

Levi was glad to see both men in such an exuberant state of mind and gave hearty approval to their plan. He had decided he was too old to stay involved with all his projects and had talked to his lawyer about freeing him up from so many obligations.

"I'll tell him to take care of you two first," he said. Looking at Barabbas, he continued, "I know you'll want to get on to Damascus."

There was a flurry of work going on in and around the shop for the next several days. Lawyers and scribes moving in and out, with Levi overseeing the results to see that the two partners' wishes were carried out.

Barabbas kept a very low profile during all this, for he did not want to be recognized or identified as the convicted tentmaker. From time to time he wondered where Faisel had gone and if he might turn up again, but he never asked and no one ever mentioned him.

At last, the details were finished. Reuben and Barabbas were unemployed and had more money than they had ever seen. Reuben promptly turned his over to Levi to invest for him. Barabbas worked out a way with Levi to be able to transfer funds to Damascus to pay what Judas owed, took two hundred pieces of silver with him, and went to see Mary and John.

He was shocked at their appearance. John had been a fisherman up near Capernaum when Jesus had called him. There was no work for fishermen around Jerusalem. The two had been somewhat withdrawn and subdued when Barabbas arrived, but when he stacked a hundred pieces of silver on the table before them, told them it was theirs and that Levi had more invested on their behalf, their joy and relief knew no bounds. Mary sat and looked at him, tears streaming down her face. And John was on his knees, head bowed in prayer.

After some minutes, John arose, approached Barabbas, embraced him, and exclaimed, "Barabbas, the Master sent you to us."

"I don't know if he did or not. I don't need the money, I'll be paid wages working for Judas. Something just told me to give it to you two. If others of the twelve are in need, there will be enough to share with them."

"That's the way the Spirit works," John replied. "If we listen, he tells us what to do. He told, you heard, and Mother Mary," he looked at her, joy and wonder in his eyes and voice, "our needs are met."

"Barabbas," Mary said, "when you knocked on the door we were at our wits end. We told Him we were hungry. There was nothing in the cupboard, and we needed some help. We thank Him so much, and I'm glad He sent you." She rose to her feet, donned her mantle, took some coins from the stack, and announced, "I'm going to the market, and you two can stay here and talk. I will be back soon." She left, humming a happy tune.

The men watched her leave, love and devotion showing in their eyes.

Barabbas cooked supper that night; Mary appeared tired, and John didn't know how. While Mary had been shopping, at the prompting of Barabbas, John began to tell what it was like to be a disciple, a follower of Jesus. Barabbas was intrigued. The recital went on during the meal, while Barabbas was cleaning up, and on until late night. Barabbas spent the night, made breakfast, and still John kept on. Barabbas soaked up the stories, the lessons, the teachings of Jesus, like a sponge. John seemed compelled to talk, and Barabbas in no way discouraged him. This was Friday, and Barabbas observed the Sabbath with them, learning more and more about the revolutionary teachings of this man who was the Son of God.

Somewhere in these three or four days and nights Barabbas wondered aloud why he had not had the privilege of being a follower like John and the others.

"Barabbas, don't you see?" Mary answered. "You had a role to play—we all did—and you played yours well. We were all born to do what we did, to be who we are. The Spirit leads us, and we have the choice to follow or not. You chose to play your role, and I'm certain God is pleased with you. Have no regrets, my friend."

Barabbas smiled, nodded, and thanked God in his heart for this woman who had played her role so willingly and well.

"I've got to go," he said. "John, I can't thank you enough for telling me about these last three years. I hope I can remember the most of it. Reuben will be wondering what's happened to me. Look in on him from time to time. He's getting some age on him. Take care of each other." The three embraced, and Mary and John followed Barabbas outside on the street.

As Barabbas reached the corner where he would turn and disappear from view, Mary called to him, "Barabbas!" He stopped, turned, and cupped his ear. "If we need to get in touch with you, where will you be?"

"I'll be in Damascus, in the house of Judas, on the street called Straight!"

CHAPTER THIRTY-EIGHT

Soon after the resurrection, the Jews who had been instrumental in the trial and conviction of Jesus saw a sudden growth in the number of followers of the Jesus Way. The disciples were fervent in their witnessing, converting more and more people to what became known simply as The Way.

To counteract this growth, these same Jews began a period of persecution against those of The Way. As a result, the more vocal and influential ones scattered far and wide, resulting in even more recruits to the movement.

When Barabbas arrived in Damascus, neither Judas nor anyone in the city had heard of the resurrection of Jesus. He and Judas harked back to the time of his birth and the report of the shepherds. Judas knew also of the time Gabriel had appeared to Joseph and of the warning about fleeing to Egypt.

He had talked to some of the people who had followed Jesus at intervals and had heard many reports of healing, restoring of sight to the blind—all kinds of miraculous things—so he was not too surprised at his coming back to life. When Barabbas explained to him the plan of God for the acceptance of God's gift of grace, Judas saw, understood, and joyfully became a member of The Way.

When some of the followers reached Damascus, they found many converts already witnessing. Barabbas had recruited brigands under cover. He found it easier and more rewarding to recruit followers of The Way out in the open.

Barabbas had been working and living with Judas for nine years on the street called Straight. The tentmaking shop was small. The two of them stayed busy, and they were content to limit their customers to what the two of them could produce.

As different people began to come by the shop in the early days of the dispersion, Barabbas's pulse would quicken and he would wonder, *Is this the one?* After a few years, that feeling of anticipation went away.

One day John came in. Many others had stopped by with news from and of Jerusalem, but John's was special. Barabbas put down his needle, thread, and cloth, and they went outside to talk. He was saddened to learn that both Mary and Reuben had died; Mary in the spring and Reuben the next winter. After John left, Barabbas disappeared for two days. He explained to Judas: "I was upset, angry at God. Did some complaining, asking why? Why? Know the answer I got?" Barabbas didn't wait for Judas to nod or shake his head. "The answer was, 'Barabbas, you can't live on earth forever. People are born to die. Accept it and look forward to it!' That's when I got smart. Having to get smart is a failing of mine." He gave

Judas a rueful smile. "Been having to do it all my life." Judas laughed at him, then suddenly sobered and began to count up to determine how old he was.

The street called Straight, as would be expected, went straight through Damascus, east and west. The house of Judas, facing Straight, was on the corner of the north-south street to the temple of Jupiter. It was dinnertime, and Barabbas and Judas had put aside their work, taken their meals, and gone to a bench outside to eat and enjoy a brief respite from their labor. This they did quite often.

Hearing an unusual sound of travel, they rose to their feet, looked south on Temple Street, and saw a contingent of ten Roman soldiers approaching. One was on horseback, the others on foot. Two of them were on either side of a blind man, holding him by his arms, carefully leading him.

Barabbas's scalp began to tingle. He looked down, saw and felt the hairs on his arms and hands standing up. *That's my man!* he thought.

The rider, apparently in charge, stopped and dismounted. Greeting them courteously, he asked, "You two live here?"

Judas nodded and answered, "We do."

Barabbas hadn't even heard the question. He was staring at his man. *Not only blind,* he told himself, *he's got a gimpy leg.*

The soldier was speaking again: "Wonder if maybe you two could help me out." He looked at Barabbas curiously, then back at Judas.

"We were escorting this man, . . ." he consulted some papers, "Saul of Tarsus, to this city on some sort of official business, and just south of here a flash of lightning came out of nowhere. He was knocked off his feet. We heard some kind of voices but couldn't understand what was said. When he got up he was blind as a bat. Hasn't spoken since. We need someone to take care of him until I can hear from my centurion in Jerusalem about what to do with him. Do you know who—?"

"We'll take care of him," interrupted Barabbas.

CHAPTER
THIRTY-NINE

They completed the arrangements with the soldier, and Barabbas led Saul inside, where he bedded him down. He lay there immobile for three days and nights. Barabbas, however, talked to him at intervals, not knowing whether or not he was heard.

"My name is Barabbas. I was a tentmaker in Jerusalem, tried and convicted of insurrection and murder and sentenced to death by crucifixion. Jesus of Nazareth, Son of God, was crucified in my place, on my cross, and I was freed after being in prison for about thirty days. Like you, I went in shock for three days. I came to my senses and met Jesus at the foot of that cross on the third day. He was alive and well, talked to me, touched me, and filled me with his Spirit. I hope he has done the same for you.

"Since then I have been a follower of his, of The Way. He wants you to be one, too. You and I both were on the wrong road. I chose to take the right one, and you have the same chance to make a choice. I hope you make the right one. If you've come this far to this point and make the wrong choice, I promise you, you will be a miserable human being. I'm going back to work. Judas and I will be near if you want or need us."

On the third day, Ananias came to the house of Judas. He had been there before, and Barabbas and Judas had been to his—the followers of The Way met often with one another. Ananias went in and talked with Saul, and when he came out Saul was with him, weak, trembling, hungry, but seeing and believing.

Barabbas and Judas prepared a big meal, and the four of them made away with it. Barabbas commented that Reuben would have said, "The man's hollow!"

After eating and drinking, Saul wanted to go out into the city and meet others of The Way, but Ananias dissuaded him.

"I knew and they know why you were coming to Damascus: to arrest and take back to Jerusalem some followers of The Way. We have heard what you have been doing elsewhere. You were holding the cloaks of those who were stoning Stephen. I was afraid of you, and they still are. I think you ought to hibernate for a while. Let us and others spread the word of your conversion."

It was then that Barabbas told them of his conversation with Gabriel, how Saul was to be taught and trained in the survival skills that could sustain him on rigorous journeys. He was also to be taught in the trade of tentmaking, to make him independent of the support of others. Barabbas went on to tell of the various appearances of Gabriel: his visit to Mary in Nazareth then to Joseph, his warnings of Herod, sending them to Egypt, on and on.

Saul listened to all this with undivided attention, as though he couldn't hear enough, learn enough. When Barabbas paused to collect his thoughts, Saul was pacing the floor in impatient excitement. "When can we leave?" he asked.

"Not until I fashion you a boot of some sort for that gimpy leg," Barabbas answered. "I didn't work all those years with Reuben for nothing. Come with me out in the shop. We'll take some measurements and see what I can come up with. The way you limp, it throws your back out of kilter. Let's see if we can't fix that."

Three days later, Judas, Ananias, and two others of The Way walked to the outskirts of the city to see Barabbas and Saul off on their trip of hibernation. Both men had loaded backpacks, each carried a staff, and Barabbas and the four well-wishers looked with approval as Saul walked jauntily along with the boot Barabbas had fashioned. He no longer looked like a bird with a broken wing. At the city gate, the little group moved off to one side, placed arms around shoulders, bowed their heads in prayer, and consigned the two travelers into God's keeping.

The three years Barabbas spent in Arabia with Saul reminded him of his years in Egypt with Mary, Joseph, and Jesus. He told Saul everything he could remember: Gabriel's visit to Mary in Nazareth, the birth of Jesus, angels and shepherds, Egypt and fishing—he talked for three years. He told of his doubts and unbelief, his work with brigands, the caravan with Faisel and Ahmed. What he would forget one day, he would recall later and fill in.

Saul was particularly interested in Mary's talk with Barabbas on the morning of the resurrection, of her faith and belief in a living Lord. And he never tired of hearing Barabbas tell of his conversion. When Barabbas told the stories the disciple John had told him, Saul was like a sponge. Saul would walk along swinging his staff and would repeat word for word things Jesus had said in John's presence.

Barabbas began to see what Gabriel meant when he said, "This man can do great things for God." When it came to Jesus and his life, he was insatiable.

The decision day finally arrived. Saul had gotten up early and had breakfast prepared when Barabbas emerged from the tent. As they were eating, Saul said to him, "Barabbas, it's time to go. I think I'm ready."

"To begin your work?"

"Yes," Saul answered. "You know," he continued, "I want to be like Jesus. I'm getting a late start and can't catch up, but I'll do the best I can. You had Jesus for three years in Egypt and trained him well. I think God in his wisdom must have had those three years with you in mind when Jesus was born." He smiled briefly.

"I said I wanted to be like Jesus. My three years with you were up yesterday, and you've taught me well. Physically, I think I can survive under the most severe conditions. You've made a man out of me. I can earn a living making tents. When I wear out a boot," he raised the foot up for inspection, "I can make another. You've filled my head, heart, and soul of stories of divine intervention. What the Lord has started on the road to Damascus, He will carry on till its ultimate conclusion. Yes, my friend, thanks to you, I'm ready."

Looking across the remaining coals of the breakfast fire, Barabbas was surprised to see the glisten of tears in the eyes of his friend and pupil. Barabbas was by nature a toucher. Many of his closest friends had been, or were still, touchers—never hesitant or ashamed to embrace or even to kiss on the cheek. With many of them, they had cried together in joy and in sorrow. Saul was not that type. He no doubt loved Barabbas, appreciated what Barabbas had done with and for him, but it was difficult for him to put those feelings into words. Barabbas had wondered if he had felt that being sentimental, shedding a tear, was a sign of weakness. That gimpy leg was still gimpy. Barabbas knew it hurt at times. He had heard him pray that it might be healed, but he had never heard him complain.

"I think, too, that you are ready," he responded. "I'm envious of what you are capable of doing and wish I was twenty years younger so that I might travel with you. John told us that Jesus said, 'Go into all the world.' I would love to tell the world what one can learn at the foot of the cross. Or on the road to Damascus." He smiled at his friend. "You'll have to tell it for me."

They both seemed lost in thought for several minutes, and Barabbas made the first move, beginning to dismantle the tent. As he did so, Saul began to assemble the packs, and soon they were moving out.

As they traveled that first day, Saul was not as voluble as he usually was, and Barabbas respected his apparent wish for introspection. In fact, Barabbas welcomed the opportunity to contemplate his own situation. He wondered if Gabriel might appear some night and give him another assignment.

At sixty-six, I don't believe I could handle another like this, he thought.

That night, they did not put up the tent, but ate early, slept lightly, and were on the road at dawn. Thus, after eight days of travel (Saul laughed when Barabbas told him the ox was in the ditch!), they arrived in Damascus and without any fanfare made their way to the house of Judas. Asking Judas not to spread any news of their return, both men went to bed, where they stayed for twenty-four hours.

The next two or three weeks were busy ones. Barabbas, Ananias, and one or two others went around the city, day and night, taking Saul with them—sometimes leaving him with Judas. They persuaded other followers of The Way that Jesus himself had spoken to Saul, had filled him with the Holy Spirit, and had enlisted him to spread the word of God's grace wherever he felt led to go. Some believed; others were skeptical. But gradually Saul's dynamic preaching began to take effect, his influence began to spread.

Meanwhile, Barabbas began to slow down. No one noticed except Judas, and he would not have been aware of any change in his demeanor but for the fact that he had known him so well for so long. That Friday night, at the beginning of the Sabbath, Barabbas went to his room and went to bed.

That night Gabriel appeared.

"Barabbas!" he called.

Barabbas opened his eyes in the darkness: "Why am I not surprised that you are here?" he asked.

Gabriel chuckled. "Wishful thinking, I suppose. Are you ready to go?"

"Yes," whispered Barabbas.

Next morning, Judas discovered that his friend and mentor had died. When Saul came in and saw him, he cried. Barabbas would have been pleased.

EPILOGUE

Barabbas was hurtling through the tunnel toward the light. The wind was rushing past, but he felt no fear. Instead, he had a peace and calmness that defied description.

He emerged from the tunnel into the light so bright it should have blinded him, but didn't. "The light the shepherds saw," he said to himself. "I see every rock, every blade of grass, every grain of sand. I'm in the presence of God!"

"Welcome, good and faithful servant. Enter into the joy of your Lord. I had just started down to the river for my daily walk with Enoch. I would like for you to join us soon. Look around for a bit, and I will see you later."

Barabbas looked toward the river and saw Enoch pacing slowly back and forth, as if waiting for someone. He looked the other direction and saw a little copse of trees nearby, a path leading that way through a grassy meadow. As he drew near, he heard the familiar *clop, clop, clop, clop* of hoofbeats, and Hiram appeared, head bobbing and tail twitching. Barabbas couldn't believe his eyes.

"Hiram, you flop-eared, long-nosed son of a jackass. You're a beautiful sight, and I'm glad to see you!"

Hiram approached, pressed his head gently against Barabbas's midsection, and turned sideways, hide rippling in pleasurable anticipation of a rubdown.

Barabbas reached into a pocket of his tunic, pulled out a piece of canvas, and began to rub the nappy hide of the donkey, calling him all kinds of derogatory names, but in a gentle, loving, affectionate tone of voice. The rippling hide and closed eyes of Hiram left no doubt but that he was enjoying the experience.

Jesus, Mary, and Joseph, standing in the shadow of the trees could hear every word. As they stepped out into the light, they looked at each other and smiled.

To order additional copies of

BARABBAS

FELON/FRIEND

send $14.99 plus $4.95 shipping and handling to

Books Etc.
PO Box 4888
Seattle, WA 98104

or have your credit card ready and call

(800) 917-BOOK